What was it about Jared Gillette that made her surrender?

He had become an uncanny force in her life, stripping her down to nagging thoughts and reckless behavior.

The reluctance with which he pulled away from their kiss was obvious. "That shouldn't have happened," he said firmly. "I live by a strict code of ethics, especially for employers and employees."

The intensity in his features, the nerve throbbing along his jaw, told her he wasn't going to back down.

"It won't happen again," he continued. "It's obvious we connect on...certain levels, but after my disastrous first marriage I promised myself no commitments, no involvements. I don't get close to anybody, Nicki. Not even you."

Nicki steeled herself, refusing to let him see how much his words hurt. "It must be a horrible way to live, Jared," she said softly. "Not ever giving anybody, not even yourself, a second chance."

"It's the way *I* live," he announced harshly. "And it will be better for both of us, to keep it that way."

Dear Reader,

What are your New Year's resolutions? I hope one is to relax and escape life's everyday stresses with our fantasy-filled books! Each month, Silhouette Romance presents six soul-stirring stories about falling in love. So even if you haven't gotten around to your other resolutions (hey, spring cleaning is still months away!), curling up with these dreamy stories should be one that's a pure pleasure to keep.

Could you imagine seducing the boss? Well, that's what the heroine of Julianna Morris's *Last Chance for Baby*, the fourth in the madly popular miniseries HAVING THE BOSS'S BABY did. And that's what starts the fun in Susan Meier's *The Boss's Urgent Proposal*— part of our AN OLDER MAN thematic series—when the boss... finally...shows up on his secretary's doorstep.

Looking for a modern-day fairy tale? Then you'll adore Lilian Darcy's *Finding Her Prince*, the third in her CINDERELLA CONSPIRACY series about three sisters finding true love by the stroke of midnight! And delight in DeAnna Talcott's I-need-a-miracle tale, *The Nanny & Her Scrooge*.

With over one hundred books in print, Marie Ferrarella is still whipping up fun, steamy romances, this time with three adorable bambinos on board in *A Triple Threat to Bachelorhood*. Meanwhile, a single mom's secret baby could lead to Texas-size trouble in Linda Goodnight's *For Her Child*..., a fireworks-filled cowboy romance!

So, a thought just occurred: Is it cheating if one of your New Year's resolutions is pure fun? Hmm...I don't think so. So kick back, relax and enjoy. You deserve it!

Happy reading!

Mary-Theresa Hussey

Mary-Theresa Hussey
Senior Editor

Please address questions and book requests to:
Silhouette Reader Service
U.S.: 3010 Walden Ave., P.O. Box 1325, Buffalo, NY 14269
Canadian: P.O. Box 609, Fort Erie, Ont. L2A 5X3

The Nanny &
Her Scrooge

DeANNA TALCOTT

SILHOUETTE *Romance*

Published by Silhouette Books

America's Publisher of Contemporary Romance

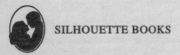

SILHOUETTE BOOKS

ISBN 0-373-19568-0

THE NANNY & HER SCROOGE

Visit Silhouette at www.eHarlequin.com

Printed in U.S.A.

Books by DeAnna Talcott

Silhouette Romance

The Cowboy and the Christmas Tree #1125
The Bachelor and the Bassinet #1189
To Wed Again? #1206
The Triplet's Wedding Wish #1370
Marrying for a Mom #1543
The Nanny & Her Scrooge #1568

DEANNA TALCOTT

grew up in rural Nebraska, where her love of reading was fostered in a one-room school. It was there she first dreamed of writing the kinds of books that would touch people's hearts. Her dream became a reality when *The Bachelor and the Bassinet*, a Silhouette Romance novel, won the National Readers' Choice award for Best Traditional Romance. That same book also earned a slot as a *Romantic Times Magazine* nominee for Best Traditional Romance, and was named as one of *Romantic Times Magazine*'s Top Picks. DeAnna's third Silhouette Romance novel, *To Wed Again?*, also won WISRWA's Readers' Choice award for Best Traditional Romance.

DeAnna claims that a retired husband, three children, two dogs and a matching pair of alley cats make her life in mid-Michigan particularly interesting. When not writing, or talking about writing, she scrounges in flea markets to indulge #1 son's quest for vintage toys, relaxes at #2 son's Eastern Michigan football and baseball games, and insists, to her daughter, that two cats simply do not need to multiply!

Dear Reader,

As the mother of a developmentally disabled child, this book, *The Nanny & Her Scrooge*, is extraspecial for me. While writing, I realized that Dominique Holliday, my heroine, represents all the wonderful people I have worked with over the years. Dominique has the patience, determination and skill to be both a parent and a friend. Her young charge, Madison, reminds me of the special children I've come to know—innocent little souls who merely seek a place to belong with people they can trust.

I have been looking a long time for a way to thank the people who have come into our lives, offering guidance, help and friendship. It has not been an easy journey, but it has been a remarkable one. Therefore, I dedicate this book to all the children who crave unconditional love and to the people who have the heart to give it.

I'd like to personally thank Residential Options for making a difference. Thank you Dominique Miller who shares her insight (as well as "loaning" me her first name for my heroine). All the ROI girls who have become part of our extended family deserve a huge thank-you: Beth, Amanda, Jessica, Cindy, Michelle, Amy, Erin, Kelley, Cyndy, Nicki and Wendi.

From Community Services for the Developmentally Disabled, a special thank-you goes out to Elizabeth E., Pam M., Andrea T. and Lehua B. Without your dedication and perseverance, this book, or any of the other books I've written in the past years, would not have been possible.

To Heartwood School...Karen, Becky, Nels, Dorothy, Barbara, Jean and a host of angels too numerous to mention...you are miracle workers, truly.

The legacy—and the memory of—Bob Shire will never be forgotten. Or that of his sidekick, Phil B. To Mrs. Sanford and Mimi S., your hearts are fashioned from gold.

To Beth B., for two decades you've listened—I call that a true friend. And to a lovable curmudgeon of a husband and two rascally sons—when the world is upside down, thank you for hanging in there and giving me the time to write.

Readers, because all these incredible people, my daughter, Afton—like Madison in my story—is moving towards her own happy ending.

DeAnna Talcott

Chapter One

Dominique Holliday jammed the pink slip into her pocket and strode into the elevator, immediately punching the sixth floor button. This made no sense, none at all. She'd gotten nothing but glowing reports from her supervisor. There had to be a mistake. There *had* to be.

Ten minutes ago she'd tried to talk to Carol, her supervisor, but the woman had looked sheepish—even uncomfortable—and turned away saying, "I'm sorry, there's nothing I can do, Nicki. Really. I got in trouble for hiring you in the first place."

A cold, hard jolt of reality sent a shiver down Nicki's spine, rattling her composure. She'd stood in the employee dressing room, wondering what she could have possibly done wrong. She'd volunteered to work overtime...she'd even taken two split shifts. There had to be a reason, but because she was a temporary employee, she knew no one *had* to tell her why they were letting her go.

It occurred to her there was only one person who could strip the power from her supervisor and hand down such an ultimatum: Jared Gillette, president and owner of Gil lette's Department Store. She'd never met Mr. Gillette, but she'd heard the rumors claiming he was the "Little Napoleon" of retail, the tyrant who ruled with an iron hand. Salesclerks quaked in their shoes when they spoke of him, merchandise buyers broke out in a sweat at the mention of his name.

When the doors of the elevator opened to the plush executive offices, Nicki tamped down her trepidation and sternly reminded herself she didn't have a choice. She had to face him. Her pocketbook demanded a little cash flow, her landlord demanded the rent.

The offices were empty. It was late, almost five o'clock on a Saturday afternoon, and because the store was located in downtown Winter Park, Gillette's closed at six on the weekends.

Nicki's trepidation grew. She felt uncomfortable for being there, as if she were trespassing.

The ominous door of Jared Gillette's executive office stared her right in the face.

So how long could it take to get this straightened out? she asked herself. Three minutes? Five? Taking a deep, fortifying breath, she marched over to the mahogany door, and raised her fist, poised to do battle. With her knuckles, she rapped three times on the satin finish.

"Yes? Come in," a deep, no-nonsense voice invited.

Nicki practically fell over backward with nerves. She grabbed the handle to steady herself, and the solid wood door rattled in its frame.

Her composure was shredded, but there was only one thing left to do: enter the chamber of horrors and have her say. She'd beg, plead, or bargain if she had to; she had to have that job.

Pushing the door a little too hard, Nicki stumbled into Jared Gillette's office. She swayed, tugged on the hem of her sweater, and tried to make her feet cooperate. When she looked up, it was into the most perceptive, deepest, darkest eyes she'd ever seen. For a split second, when Jared Gillette's inquisitive gaze collided with hers, she couldn't tear herself away. Something needy and profound spiraled right down into the pit of her soul.

He was younger than she'd imagined—maybe thirty-five—and far too handsome. His hair was as shiny and polished as onyx, and his wide forehead and high cheekbones appeared sculpted of alabaster. His mouth was full, and his nose was straight and wide. Impeccably dressed in a dark, pin-striped suit, Jared Gillette's scarlet tie was perfectly knotted between the points of a crisp white collar. At his wrists, gold cuff links winked at her.

Nicki imperceptibly closed her eyes and shook herself, as if she could fling his disturbing features from being imprinted on her memory.

"Mr. Gillette..." she began unsteadily, forcing herself to meet his eyes.

"Yes," he confirmed sharply, setting aside a sheaf of papers, "I am. And you would be?"

"Dominique Holliday. I—I work for Gillette's Department Store...or at least I did until an hour ago." Nicki fumbled in her pocket, to find the termination letter. She extended the crumpled paper in his direction. "I've tried to talk to my supervisor, but she says there's nothing she can do...so I thought, maybe you could—"

He scowled at her, waiting.

A feeling of helplessness surged through Nicki. "Look," she said defiantly, "I was hired two weeks ago by Carol Whitman as a Santa Claus because she knew I could work with kids, and I've bent over backward to do my job. I'm the best Santa Claus on the floor, and I don't understand this. Not at all."

"Oh," was all he said. The pause was positively pregnant. "You're the one."

"You fired me?" she asked, her voice rising with disbelief. "You don't even know me."

"Miss—" he brazenly skimmed her length "—whatever your name is—"

"Nicki. Nicki Holliday," she repeated.

"Yes. Well, we have very strict criteria for our Santa Clauses and you've obviously failed to meet—"

"What do you mean," she nearly wailed. "I've done everything right. I'm happy, I'm jolly. I have the best 'ho, ho, ho' in the entire Santa Claus fleet." For a split second she was certain she saw the corner of his mouth start to twitch. "I do. You can ask anybody. Here. Let me demonstrate—"

Jared raised a hand, effectively stopping her. "No. Please don't," he said curtly. "It's late, and this has not been a holly-jolly, ho-ho-ho day."

Nicki stared at him. "No kidding? Well, getting fired sure dampens my Christmas spirit, too."

"Miss, um, Holliday—" He suddenly snorted, as if the significance of her surname struck him. "Gillette's is the largest department store in southern Indiana. Our clients expect certain things—"

"Like?"

"Like a *Mr.* Santa Claus, not a Mrs."

He'd fired her because she was a *woman?* Nicki started shaking, knowing there was nothing she could do about that. "I've done everything possible to present a plausible image of Santa to your customers and their children," she implored. "None of them finds me lacking. None of the children even suspect."

He chuckled, and his dark gaze nailed her. "Miss Holliday, look at yourself. Your eyes may twinkle and, with a little makeup, you might have a nose like a cherry. But I really doubt—really—that your belly's going to jiggle like a bowlful of jelly."

Heat prickled across the back of her neck. "Padding," she retorted, "lots of it."

Nicki thought she saw a flicker of amusement hover behind his eyes. Then his attitude changed—abruptly.

"No," he said firmly, picking up the letter he'd been reading at her untimely entrance. "Santa Clauses are jolly old grandpas with wrinkled skin and bushy eyebrows. They are not young women who have to gird themselves with padding and lower their voices two octaves."

"If you'd just give me a chance—"

"This matter is not open to discussion. Period. Being a Santa Claus for Gillette's is out of the question, so forget it. I'm sure you can see yourself out—especially since you did such a fine job of seeing yourself in."

Nicki's cheeks flamed and her hands shook. "You can't fire me because I'm a woman," she finally managed to blurt.

His head lifted, lionlike. His dark eyes glittered and his features were taut, as if he were ready to go in for the kill. "Like hell I can't."

Nicki caught her breath.

"Now get out of my office."

She thought she was going to die right then and there. Just fade away into oblivion under the merciless gaze of Jared Gillette. Then it occurred to her: what did she have to lose? "I—I...really didn't mean to impose on you or your time," she said. Lacing her fingers together, she held them taut against her middle. She couldn't give up, not now. "Keeping this job is really important to me, Mr. Gillette, and I'm sure if you checked my track record...you'd see...." She let the rest go unsaid.

He sat back. For a moment she wasn't sure if he was glaring at her or considering her suggestion. Then his gaze drifted down to her trembling hands.

Dammit! Why'd he have to notice? Couldn't he let her writhe in agony without giving her one of those looks? Frustration set in, making her eyelids burn and her vision grow watery. Nicki feared that if she blinked, a tear would dribble from the corner of her eye.

"Okay. Look," he said in exasperation, thwacking the papers beside him. "If you want to be an elf, you can be an elf. You're about the right size anyway."

"I..." She hesitated, very much aware he was making a concession. "No. It has to be the Santa Claus job."

He pulled back, as if appalled she'd have the audacity to insist.

"Impossible. This time around, Santa Claus is definitely gender based. If you want to come back at Easter and be a bunny...."

"That's four months away," Nicki protested, taking a step toward him. "And right now I'm doing my absolute best to be realistic and genuine. Parents love me, children flock to me. There hasn't been one complaint—not one— and if you'd only stop by to watch me, and see how I relate to the kids—"

"Miss Holliday. I don't have time for that. It's an elf or nothing."

Deflation oozed through Nicki, numbing her mind and every logical argument. As her eyes shuttered closed, imagining the debt and the dilemma she was in, she glimpsed Jared Gillette. The man was heartless, with eyes like flint and misplaced conviction where compassion should be. Forget the good looks, he was Scrooge incarnate. "It won't do," she said flatly, "I can't be an elf."

"Fine. We don't need you. Pick up your check in the office. If you change your mind, then—"

"No," Nicki interrupted, "It's more complicated than that."

"Miss Holliday. I don't care how complicated it is. The choice is yours, do as you wish. Now, if there's nothing else, get out of my office and close the door behind you. I have work to do."

Nicki stared at him, then she turned and fled.

All in all, it had been an interesting day, Jared mused, closing Nicki Holliday's personnel file. His morning hadn't gotten off to a particularly good start. A new employee had unwittingly brought out a cart of the most sought-after doll in Christmas history and caused a near riot in the toy department. Later, one shopper had had an allergic reaction to fragrances in the cosmetics department and the paramedics had rushed in the front doors with a stretcher. Aside from the three "lost" children and one wandering Alzheimer's patient, they'd also caught three shoplifters.

And then there had been Nicki Holliday...the woman who had pretty effectively, according to this file, passed herself off as Santa Claus.

He had to admit that her eyes *had* twinkled. In fact, she had the bluest, most fascinating eyes he'd ever seen. He could imagine a youngster leaning into her, confiding their deepest, innermost desires.

If eyes were the windows to the soul, her gaze had offered up nothing but blind trust. He'd looked into her eyes for but a moment and nearly forgotten who he was and what his intentions were. It had taken all he had to remind himself—and her—he had a job to do.

Nicki Holliday was a pretty woman. Her cheeks were plump, with identical dimples that took on a life of their own, playing peek-a-boo with him during their entire conversation. Her hair—brilliant, shiny shades of nutmeg, cinnamon, and ginger—actually reminded him of the Christmas potpourri in Gillette's Home for the Holidays section. Funny. She reminded him of the strangest things. Of comforting things.

He wondered, vaguely, if the gray Santa wig and beard could convincingly cover her short, tousled dark hair, or age her peaches-and-cream complexion. Probably not. She had an ethereal quality, one that would just shine through the costume and makeup anyway.

So? What did it matter? There was no way he was having a female—any female—play the part of Santa Claus.

Some things simply were. Santa Claus was a man, not a woman. He had a great big belly, not a size six waist. He wore a red costume and sported a white beard, and he didn't have to lower his voice to fool anybody. Those were the things his customers had come to expect. It was a given, and he intended to give them what they wanted.

He, Jared Gillette, a mere businessman in middle America, was not about to trifle with tradition. Santa Claus was a legendary hero, idolized by young and old alike. Jared refused to take any kind of creative license with something of those proportions.

Still…he had experienced a glimmer of regret when he witnessed Nicki's disappointment. If it was just the job….

He shook his head, staunchly reminding himself he had made the right decision, even if her file had verified that she'd been a virtual hit with both parents and kids. Too bad. Some things were simply not meant to be.

Glancing at the clock, he realized everyone had gone home, and he would be closing up the store again. Just him and security. Just as usual.

Pulling on his overcoat, he walked over to the window. The street traffic was almost nonexistent. It had started snowing again and, if the frost on the window was any indication, the temperature had dropped drastically. Grabbing his briefcase, he headed for the elevator, estimating there'd be just enough time to run home to change.

On the first floor in the subdued lighting of the empty store, Joe, the old codger of a security guard, nodded and held open the front door. "You workin' late again, boss?"

"It's Christmas," Jared explained unnecessarily, never breaking his stride.

"I know, I know. Busiest time of the year." Joe propped the door open with his shoulder, and hitched up the pants on his blue uniform.

Pausing on the sidewalk, Jared yanked his collar up against the bitter cold. He hadn't gone twenty paces in the direction of the parking ramp when he saw her—Nicki Holliday—standing at the bus stop, her back against the wind. In a light summer-weight jacket, she shivered, both hands jammed into her pockets.

For a moment it occurred to him that he should nod and

just keep walking. Then she looked up and saw him. Their gazes caught and held. Jared's brisk pace imperceptibly slowed. Something about the way she stood there, all alone, with snow dusting her hair, twisted his heart. "Miss Holliday? You're still here?"

She nodded, hunching her shoulders. "I guess I stayed too long in your office. I missed my bus."

He pulled back his sleeve to check his watch. "The seven o'clock bus isn't scheduled for at least another forty minutes. If it comes at all. Weekends are kind of hit or miss."

"Okay, well—" Nicki's teeth chattered "—thanks for the warning. I'll figure out something."

She didn't say one word about their run-in, and that in itself was unsettling. Jared took one step past her, thought better of it, and turned on his heel. "Listen, why don't I give you a ride home?"

"Oh, no. Forget that. I'm fine."

"Fine? You're practically blue."

The wind gusted, plastering the thin satin jacket against Nicki's shoulders. "No, it's okay." She tried to smile. "Hey, I'm Santa Claus. I've called the North Pole and they've assured me I'll have a sleigh gliding by momentarily. I'll grab a little milk and cookies at the diner down the street and wait. If they're late, it's because Donder's probably acting up again. He does that."

He didn't reply, only stared at her, vaguely wondering if she even had a home to go to. Maybe she was a nutcase.

"Ho, ho, ho," she feebly joked, "then off I'll go. Into my sleigh, and over the snow."

With an inexplicable surge of impatience, Jared dismissed her rhyme and looked over her shoulder, down the street. Every storefront was dark, and the diner she mentioned was a good two blocks away. "Look. It's dark, it's cold, and you're half frozen. If you start telling me you actually live at the North Pole, I'm going to think you're delirious to boot."

She laughed, a tinkly little sound that reverberated through the darkness. "Okay. I can assure you I'm not delirious, and I don't live at the North Pole. What you just witnessed is my kid-appeal. I wanted to wedge it in while I had your full attention."

She was making references to the ill-fated job, and Jared pursed his lips, choosing to ignore them. "Miss Holliday, I insist on driving you home."

"No. That's okay."

"Do you realize," he asked, "that I'm trying to do you a favor? Perhaps because I feel somewhat responsible for you missing your ride."

She stopped shivering and gazed at him, with liquid, clear blue eyes, as if she were shocked he admitted any culpability at all. "Why? Because you altered the Santa 'clause' of my job?"

He didn't reply. "Come on," he ordered, "my car's right inside the parking garage."

She stayed rooted to the spot.

He turned back, lifting his eyebrows with the unspoken question.

"I don't want to put you out," she said.

It struck him how there was not a hint of malice in her voice. He'd expected it, guessed he even deserved it. She stood there, looking a little forlorn, her hair all tousled, her cheeks chapped from the bitter wind, and simply met his gaze. Yet there wasn't a bit of recrimination in her features.

This woman, ephemeral as the snow, was unsettling. She preyed on his protective instincts, making him want to toss a warm coat around her shoulders and press a hot chocolate into her hand. Even in this bitter cold, he'd rather idle with her on a street corner than leave her here.

"You aren't putting me out," he said too softly, aware the wind pulled at his words and carried them away. He hesitated, raised his voice, and assumed the stance of a dictator. "You're either going to come with me, or I'm going to stay here with you, until I'm sure you're on that bus."

"If it doesn't come at all, you're in for a long wait."

"Come on," he said, reaching into his coat pocket and pulling out his car keys. "Let's go."

Without any pretense or further objection, she lowered her head into the wind and followed him.

It was a mere fifty feet to his Lincoln, the doors were unlocked and the engine running before they entered the parking ramp. Thank God for remote control. He could get a little heat into her, get another color other than blue onto her lips.

"Thank you," she said humbly as he held the door for her.

"It isn't a courtesy," he snapped. "Your fingers are probably too frozen to open the door."

She slipped into the passenger seat, then proved his point by fumbling with the seat belt. Snagging it from her, he righted the buckle, and offered it back, intending to make it manageable. Their fingertips brushed; a ping of electricity ricocheted up his arm.

Startled, they both pulled back.

Jared straightened and, still looking at her, hung an elbow on the top of the car door. "Miss Holliday, can you tell me something? Why can't you just be an elf and make this easier on me? I know what you're trying to do. Really. And it's not going to work. I promise you, it's not going to work. I deal with people like you every day of the week—and guess what?—I'm the grinch who eats them up and spits them out."

Chapter Two

Jared's statement incensed Nicki, but she waited until he'd tossed his briefcase into the back seat and got into the car before answering. "I'm not trying to do anything," she denied. "And just call me Nicki. It's not like we have to be formal or anything. Because I don't work for you. Not anymore. I wouldn't work for you if you were the last man on earth."

He arched an eyebrow in her direction, his mouth a hard firm line as he carefully put the key into the ignition. "Look. Do you need a job or not?" he barked.

"Of course, I need a job. Everybody needs a job. To pay the bills, to make the mortgage and the car payments and to eat."

He snagged a deep, angry breath, nearly scaring Nicki. She put her hand on the door handle, debating whether she should bolt.

"If that's the case, then why won't you swallow your pride and accept the one I've offered you?"

She slanted him a look, gauging his reaction. "Because I don't like those hideous green tights and that goofy hat with the bells," came her flip reply. "I'd feel like an idiot wearing that get-up."

He sat back and considered, then his mouth twitched and the creases eased from his forehead. He actually laughed. Out loud.

The resonant sound filled the car, unexpectedly warming Nicki and putting some of her fears to rest. Okay, anybody who laughed like that couldn't be all bad, she conceded.

He dragged a hand over his face, as if the joke were unbearable. "And you don't feel like an idiot wearing a red velvet Santa suit, slapping a beard on your face, and shouting ho, ho, ho?" he finally asked.

He had her there, and the irony of the situation made her squirm. "Okay, I'll admit that at the time, I figured it was worth it."

"What?"

"The job. The money," she explained wearily, slumping down in the plush seat. "My car died a month ago. It's going to take a lot of money for repairs."

"So that's why you were stranded tonight."

"I've been able to take the bus, but tonight I spent so much time in your office I missed the one at five o'clock. Since I didn't really have anyone to call..." Nicki let the statement drift, she didn't want to admit she couldn't afford a cab, or didn't have anyone to pick her up.

"So about this elf thing..." he began.

"Forget it. I already talked to the supervisor about that. The elves are typically teenagers and they only do four-hour shifts. Right now, they have too many, anyway."

"I see."

Nicki rubbed her arms and shrugged. "No, you don't."

His head swiveled and he glanced at her sharply, as if daring her to contradict him.

She gnawed on her lower lip and tried to not shiver in his presence. The last thing she wanted was for him to think she was afraid of him. She wouldn't give him that. She wouldn't. "I needed a job where I could make some good money in a short amount of time. A good Santa makes a respectable salary, but the elves are gofers who mostly fill the candy-cane jar and make minimum wage, and sales-clerks don't make much more, so that's out.'' She stuck her hands under her arms, trying in vain to warm them. "I don't know. The Santa pay is really good. Maybe there's a union label sewn in the Santa suit or something.''

He paused, his features relaxing. "Cute—about the union label. But the fact is the Santa job takes a certain type of person, that's why it pays so well.''

Nicki studied him briefly, acutely conscious that a portion of his tough-businessman facade had slipped. It made her feel as though a real man existed beneath that intimidating demeanor.

As if it had a will of its own, her hand fluttered across the empty space between them to settle apologetically on his sleeve. "I understand why you felt the way you did about having a grandpa Santa Claus,'' she explained softly. "But as I mentioned earlier, I needed to get my car fixed, and I'm expecting to move. It takes money to do that. It's that simple, really. I'm not trying to buck the system or to cause you problems or even to argue with you.''

He silently stared at her, then dropped his gaze to her fingers that still curled lightly on his forearm. Without shaking her off, he slowly started the ignition. "Why didn't you tell me that this afternoon?''

Nicki self-consciously slid her hand away, but the feel of cashmere taunted her fingers, and the restrained power throbbing through his muscular forearm sent a surge of exhilaration to her brain. She folded her hands in her lap. "You never gave me the opportunity.''

His mouth firmed and he put the car in gear. They were inching onto the adjacent one-way street when he said, "You didn't tell me where we were going.''

"Tammany Hills. I'm just a few doors inside the complex.'' Another chill struck Nicki and she fought to repulse it. She stiffened and folded her arms across her middle, thinking she didn't want to explain why, after six months, she still had a Florida wardrobe, a broken-down car, and a financial mess. Her mother had been so sick when she'd finally given up and called her home, all Nicki had had time to do was to care for her mom and ignore the repercussions of her abrupt move. She'd lost a ton of money and incurred a lot of expenses.

"Tammany's a nice place," he commented, easing onto the east-west expressway.

She shrugged and glanced out the side window at the residential area next to the highway. There were moments, such as this, when she glimpsed a decorated tree inside someone else's living room, and felt like an orphan at Christmas. She'd always heard the first year was the worst. "Mmm. Expensive. But the lease is up in a couple of months. It was actually my mom's place."

"Nicki…"

She pulled her gaze away, tucking her chin to look up at Mr. Gillette. In the half light of the dash, his features were less imposing. Her eyes lowered to his mouth, and for one crazy moment she wondered what it would be like to kiss him. To experience an unguarded side of him. When he'd accidentally touched her—

"About today," he went on, unknowingly interrupting her wayward thoughts, "I assumed that you were interested only in a seasonal job. Or a part-time job. If you want a real job, I could probably find you something."

Her shoulders immediately lifted off the seat. The last thing she wanted was charity. Especially from someone who had dismissed her barely two hours before. "Oh, no. I'm not looking for a handout. You don't have to be nice to me just because this whole situation is…well, awkward."

"'Nice'?" The word harshly rolled off his tongue. "Nicki, understand this, I'm not known for nice. Not even in the most awkward of business situations."

"Well, I'll think about it…but…" She turned back to

glance out the side window again. She felt a little sad inside—and she knew it didn't have anything to do with losing her job, or her mom, or all the rest of it. Maybe it was letting go of the illusion. Maybe it was because she was trapped inside a car with a man who obviously didn't understand the meaning of Christmas. "You know," she said softly, wistfully, "I really liked being a Santa Claus. I liked being with the kids—that was the best. And the fantasy—especially the one you create at Gillette's—was all so hopeful, so innocent. Sitting there in Toyland, waving and wishing everyone a merry Christmas made me feel good inside."

"It's just that. A fantasy," he said abruptly, before leaning over and turning up the heat.

Defeat spiraled through her; he didn't even want to know how the job had affected her.

He checked his side mirror, then changed lanes, expertly maneuvering around another slower car. "I read your file this afternoon," he said. "You apparently had a knack for making people believe."

"Maybe I wanted to. A little Christmas gift to myself this year."

His gaze flitted over her, but he said nothing. For a mile, they rode in silence.

Nicki was extraordinarily conscious of him. The scent clinging to his cashmere coat. The leather gloves he'd laid between them on the seat. The way he sat so straight, so erect, as he drove.

"Listen," he said, "I live over there, off of Willow. Do you object to me stopping at home first and changing my clothes?" Nicki knew he was referring to the posh section of Winter Park. "I have to make an obligatory appearance at the Yuletide Gala tonight, at the Ritz Carlton, and I'm already late. I could drop you off on the way."

Even though she didn't want to spend any more time with him than necessary, Nicki was curious about where he lived. Besides, there was no sense in going home to an empty apartment any sooner than she had to. "That's fine."

"You're sure?"

"As you said, Mr. Gillette, you're the one doing me the favor."

He raised an eyebrow at her. "I imagine your insolence didn't put you in good favor with the elves. That's probably the real reason you didn't want to join their ranks."

"Mr. Gillette—"

"Excuse me," he cut in, as he smoothly pulled off the expressway and into the right-hand lane. "There is an unwritten rule…"

"Yes?"

"Anyone I invite into my home has to call me Jared."

Nicki's breath caught behind her breastbone. "You haven't invited me into your home."

He braked at the stop sign, and turned his head to look at traffic before he looked at her. "No. But I'm going to."

The slow smile that inched onto Jared's face sapped the remainder of Nicki's waning strength.

Jared's palatial home occupied at least a quarter of the block. Nicki glimpsed the front of the sprawling brick mansion when he came in off a side street and passed through the wrought-iron gates. It struck her as odd that the grounds had been exquisitely decorated for Christmas; for some reason, she didn't think he'd bother.

Garland, with red bows, trimmed the iron fencing. A huge wreath hung over the four-car garage, and flickering candles illuminated every window in the house.

"My," she murmured, "this is Christmas-card perfect."

"And none of my doing," he pointed out darkly. "It's just another illusion I have to live with, and I promise you it's quite unlike what you experienced as a Santa Claus in Toyland."

Nicki didn't have time to consider the telling statement because he led her inside through the back door and immediately steered her into the family room. She gaped up at the cathedral ceiling, and the second-floor balcony. Dwarfed by the proportions, she offhandedly guessed this one room was larger than her mother's entire town house.

"My folks built this house, and the floor plan's a little dated, a little cut up. But the kitchen's through the butler's pantry, in there," he said. "Help yourself."

Nicki followed the direction he indicated. She waved off his suggestion, figuring she'd get lost if she tried to negotiate one more room.

"Suit yourself," he said, peeling off his overcoat to throw it over the back of a chair. He hit the light switch, illuminating the fireplace. "Make yourself comfortable, I'll only be a minute."

She nodded, "Thank you."

He took a couple of steps, then paused, fiddling with his cuff links to remove them.

Nicki glanced over at him, transfixed. There was something about a man and his cuff links...the way his fingers worked at removing them, the way he turned back the cuffs, covering the thick bones of his wrists and exposing the dark hairs across the backs of his hands. She looked up, startled to realize he'd caught her watching. An odd, almost bemused expression shadowed his gaze. He slipped the cuff links into his pants' pocket.

"If you're still cold, I've got an afghan." He pulled a chenille throw off the leather couch.

Nicki rubbed her arms and tried to protest that she'd be fine, but for an instant she was afraid this unexpected chill of awareness didn't have a thing to do with the cold. She was acutely conscious she was in his home, alone, with him. The man-woman thing wrought unexpected havoc with her senses.

He shook open the throw for her. "Here. I can see you don't know how to dress for the weather." Instead of offering it to her, he moved behind her to slide the afghan over her shoulders.

Heat seeped through the afghan, in all the places his hands had touched. Her heart yammered.

"Actually," she said, accepting the ends from him, "these are my Florida clothes."

"Florida?"

"Oh, long story," she said dismissively, pulling the afghan tighter around her. "And not a particularly interesting one, not when you're already late."

He backed away, never taking his eyes off her. "I'll just be a few minutes. As I said, make yourself comfortable."

Nicki nodded and turned back into the room. She could hear his distinctive tread behind her on the carpet. When she knew he was out of the room, she walked over to the floor-to-ceiling windows, and tried to not shiver. Garden lights illuminated a winding path off the deck. At the end of the path was a gazebo where a huge Christmas tree glittered beneath a veil of carefully spaced colored lights.

It was obvious that everything had been professionally decorated. She chuckled, in spite of herself, wondering how it must be to be Jared Gillette and have everyone provide you with a Christmas.

Turning from the window, she nearly bumped into the grand piano.

"Wow…" she whispered, trailing a hand over the gold ribbon and greenery on the top. Interspersed in the arrangement were framed photos of a wide-eyed cherub with a pouty mouth, a flirtatious brow, and a riot of long, blond hair. Nicki reached over to carefully extract a photo. This child was a darling…and she'd seen her fair share of kids the past few weeks.

She didn't think Jared was married. Maybe a niece? Cousin? Family friend, or godchild?

Carefully placing the photo back, she strolled to the other side of the room and tarried at the fireplace mantel. Black-and-white snapshots of a younger Jared and his friends scattered the length. All were framed, many were inscribed.

She sniffed. Obviously there was a different side of Jared

Gillette than she was familiar with. These snapshots made the man actually seem human.

She was about to turn away when something caught her eye. A tiny pair of baby shoes, obviously worn, the white leather creased, the toes scuffed and the laces a bit dirty. She couldn't help it, she picked up one shoe and found an inscription in black felt-tip marker on the sole. *J.G.'s 1st pair of shoes.*

Jared Gillette was actually this little once? He hadn't always been a larger-than-life tyrant?

Smiling to herself, Nicki straightened the loops on one of the bows and carefully set the shoe aside. She wandered further down the mantel and discovered a grass-stained baseball encased in a plastic cover. *1st Home Run, Little League, Jared G., Age 11.* Next to it, a wooden car along with a tiny plastic trophy, also housed in a plastic case, were identified with a gold plate. *1st Place, Pinewood Derby, Winter Park Cub Scout Pack #47.* Further along, there was a brown-speckled rock, an autographed Indiana University baseball schedule, and a silver baby spoon.

Nicki stood back, surveying the collection of odds and ends. Jared Gillette, she thought, this is your life. You may be a hard-nosed businessman, but you definitely have another, much more curious, dimension.

Next to the mantel were two exquisitely framed watercolors. She stood for a moment, studying them.

"Like them?" Jared asked, coming up behind her. "This was my mom's retreat and she had only her favorite family things in here. I keep telling myself I should dump the personal stuff and stick to only a few good pieces of art."

Nicki whirled, ashamed to be caught looking. "They're…" The words died in her throat. The image he presented took her breath away. He was wearing a midnight-black tuxedo. He'd replaced the scarlet business tie with a crisp, formal black bow tie. His pleated dress shirt sported black studs for buttons and there were heavy gold links at his shirt cuffs. He fiddled with one link, adjusting it beneath his jacket sleeve.

Then he caught her glance and lifted a brow, offering her a mind-bending smile. "Yes?"

"The watercolors are beautiful," she said, fighting to keep her composure. "Keep them."

His laugh was short, brittle. "Funny. I thought you were going to say something else."

She hesitated. "I was. Seeing you dressed up like that, reminded me of only one thing. A grinch in a penguin suit."

His brows lifted in surprise, then he threw back his head and laughed, not the least bit irked at her audacity.

Nicki caved in and actually felt herself smiling. Then she chuckled, her laughter mingling with his in the cavernous room. She slipped the afghan from her shoulders and started to fold it, even as she shook her head, marveling at what had just transpired. "Okay. That's good. For both of us," she admitted, replacing the afghan on the back of the leather couch. "A little laugh at the end of a bad day. We may never be business associates, but at least we can laugh about our differences. And by the way, I'm sorry for that crack I made about not working for you if you were the last man on earth. It's bothered me that I said that. I overreacted, and I know it."

Jared's laughter faded and he grew silent. His gaze settled on the top of her windblown hair, then ricocheted between her dimples. The woman had an uncanny knack for amusing him. She was bright, articulate, and remarkably attractive. On top of that, she was sincere.

"Nicki Holliday...you are the most—" The phone rang, interrupting him. He blinked. "Give me a minute..."

He picked up the phone and never had time to offer up the customary "Hello?" Sandra, his ex-wife, launched into her spiel. Even from four steps away, he guessed Nicki could hear her demanding voice. He turned his back. "Sandra...of course, I'll take her...." While his ex-wife rambled on, Jared was vaguely conscious that Nicki had discreetly moved to the other side of the room. "Then we better do something about joint custody," he said.

Could he actually turn this around to his advantage? He'd been waiting a long time—and patience had never been his virtue. His lawyer had predicted this day would come.... But Jared could already see through the ruse: his ex-wife was throwing up a smokescreen to get him to up the ante.

Pulling the phone away from his ear, he made a snap decision. He didn't care what it cost, he wanted his child back.

Snagging a deep breath, he wedged the phone back against his ear, to endure Sandra's screeching. "Madison doesn't like Howie, and they pick on each other like a couple of little kids—"

"Fine. I'll have my lawyer contact yours tomorrow."

"But you're still single, Jared, and you spend all your time at that stupid store. Madison needs a real home, a feminine influence. I know you, you'll just dump her and forget her. She needs a woman around."

Jared's eye fell on Nicki, and suddenly the most outrageous idea struck him. Hell, he could bend the truth a little; his ex-wife had been doing it for the past ten years. "Actually, Sandra, I'm currently involved in a very serious relationship. She's here right now. But...look...don't say anything to Madison, will you? I'll tell her when the time is right."

He was met with dead silence on the other end of the line. Finally, "You?" Sandra accused. "And another woman?"

"Not with just anyone," he said, thinking of Nicki in a Santa suit. "This is someone who cares. Someone who loves kids. She's a nice woman. You'd like her."

"Well, I..."

"Sandra, look...we'll settle this."

"I don't care when it's settled," Sandra hissed. "Because I'm sending Madison out to you. Whether you like it or not.''

"I'll arrange for her airline ticket," Jared said smoothly, aware Sandra didn't spend one cent of the child support he sent her on Maddy. She spent it all on herself.

When Jared finally dropped the phone back into the cradle, disbelief washed through him. After all these years he was getting his child back. Even if it was only part-time—for now.

Across the room, Nicki, silhouetted against a wall of windows, half turned in his direction. She frowned, concern written on her features. "Everything okay?" she asked.

"Never better," he assured. He paused for a moment and straightened his jacket before moving toward Nicki. He had to make a decision and he had to make it quickly. "Would it be easier," he asked bluntly, "for you to walk away from the Santa job, if I offered you a Santa-like job?"

She stared at him. "Are you serious?"

"Absolutely. You'd work here. In my home. With a pay raise substantially more than anything an elf could ever possibly make. I'd certainly match the Santa pay, and probably throw in a little extra. Actually, a lot extra."

Surprise turned to suspicion. "Doing what?"

"Taking care of the most precocious little girl in the whole world."

"Who?" she asked, frowning.

"My daughter. Madison."

Nicki stalled, visibly weighing the implications. "Jared..." she said carefully, "you don't even know me."

"I know enough to know you'd be perfect for the job," he stated. "And I need somebody right away. There're twenty-nine days until Christmas, and this is not the ideal time for me to find a nanny." He strode over to the baby grand and plucked the most whimsical portrait out of the display. He extended it to her. "Nicki, meet my daughter Madison. My ex, after two years, has decided she's had enough. She's giving me joint custody—and it's the best

Christmas present I could have asked for.'' Jared unconsciously reached for her upper arm, persuasively squeezing it. ''Nicki, think about this. You need a job, I need the help. Come on. Let's make a deal.''

Chapter Three

Nicki agreed to talk about it on the way home. But in the car, she waffled. She liked Jared—almost more than she should. Yet she knew how he was when it came to business, how would he be when it came to family?

"You're perfect for the job, Nicki. I read your personnel file. You're a whiz with the kids. There were a dozen parents who called the store complimenting you."

"Seeing a child for five minutes is a lot different than being a full-time baby-sitter."

"You've got the imagination to handle it."

"But there would be a lot involved—"

"Only Madison. Irene has been my housekeeper for years. She cooks, she cleans, she even does the laundry. She runs my place with an iron hand."

"Oh, good," Nicki said dryly. "Then I'd get to put up with two of you."

Jared's sensuous mouth twitched, but he stared straight ahead at the road. "Irene is efficient, she's not an ogre."

Nicki worried the strap of her purse, debating "I don't know...your hours for the next few weeks will be long."

"That's why I need someone reliable. I don't have a lot of time to invest, and I have to make this work."

"It's going to be an adjustment for Madison. Especially if you aren't going to be home very much. Maybe you should hire someone more experienced, more…" She lifted both shoulders, at a loss for words.

"Nicki, I've seen nothing but praise where you're concerned. Your background check has already been done for the Santa Claus job, so I know nothing criminal or unsavory is lurking in your past. Reliable help is hard to find, and I need someone right away—someone I can trust."

"But why does it have to be me?" she nearly wailed.

He stopped at a traffic light, tapping his fingers impatiently against the steering wheel. "Aside from all the other reasons, you convinced me you believe in Christmas. This year I have to make it special. I want someone who can make my house smell like gingerbread and who can pick out and wrap the perfect presents for a five-year-old. Come on…" He wheedled. "I know you've got the inside track on that one."

Nicki's head fell back against the headrest. "Sunny, the power print doll, and Curious Kendall, the electronic board game," she intoned.

"See?" he said, depressing the accelerator, "I haven't spent enough time with Madison in the last few years to know those things. I need someone—maybe a *Saint* 'Nick'—to make us a family again."

Nicki rolled her head over, to study Jared's silhouette and ponder this new predicament. "You aren't playing fair," she said. "You're using my arguments against me."

If he only knew what he was doing to her. She had been dreading Christmas, maybe that was why she had been giving her all at work. Without her mom, she was alone—and what Nicki wanted more than anything was a family.

But Jared Gillette wasn't offering her that, she sternly reminded herself. He was offering her the opportunity to be hired help to *his* family.

"The thing is, I'd still have transportation problems," she said.

Jared's response was lightning-quick. "Not if you move in."

Nicki's jaw dropped.

"I have seven bedrooms and six baths. I think we could find you something comfortable. Maybe the guest room," he said thoughtfully, "it has a sitting room and an efficiency kitchen."

"Oh, why are you doing this to me," she moaned.

"What?"

Grimacing, Nicki tried to dredge up one more argument. There weren't any; there were only positives to this arrangement. Her mom always said things happened for a reason. Maybe this was a time to remember and to embrace mom's sage old advice.

"My mom's lease is up at the end of January, and I'd been trying to find something—" she hesitated, ashamed to admit her dire predicament "—less expensive. But if you think that we could manage to get along, in the same house, and not..."

"I do," Jared said firmly.

For some strange reason his response rattled Nicki. He made it sound as if they were taking vows, not agreeing to a business deal. "Okay," she said reluctantly. "I've got my reservations, but since this is just a temporary arrangement, you've got a baby-sitter."

A smug smile settled onto Jared's features. He slowed at the entrance to Tammany Hills and flipped on the turn signal. "You're on the clock," he said. "Starting now."

"Now?" Nicki couldn't keep the ripple of surprise from her voice.

"Mmm-hmm."

"Oh, that one, to the right," she directed, as he turned into the complex. "The gray front with the red shutters and trim." She took a deep breath. "I can't do it that quickly. I need to get my life in order."

He pulled up into the assigned parking space. "Get your life in order tomorrow," he scowled. "Tonight, you put on your dancing shoes and wear something dressy. I want you with me at this charity event."

Nicki's jaw slid off center. "But...but...but—" Realizing that she sounded like a motor running out of steam, her mouth whomped shut.

He shut off the car and turned to her, resting an elbow over the back of the seat. He skimmed her front with a challenging look, as if daring her to balk.

"Here's the deal," he said flatly. "I told my ex-wife that she wouldn't have to worry about Maddy, because I have a new woman in my life, one who will be able to help me out and do all the little-girl things." He shrugged. "For some reason she seemed extraordinarily concerned about that." He nailed her with a telling glance. "Guess what? That woman is you."

A feeling of anticipation and dread pooled in Nicki's middle. Her mouth went watery, and for an instant she wondered if she'd truly lost her mind to even consider working for this man. Aside from the entire scenario being preposterous, Jared made her jittery, as if she were being pulled in two directions.

"If I know my ex," Jared went on, "she'll call someone tomorrow to find out who I escorted to the gala. You're going to play the part of the woman in my new, serious relationship, and you're going to help me get full custody."

"I can't," she protested. "That seems so...deceitful. Dishonest."

"Not if you know my ex-wife," he said brusquely.

Nicki shook her head, debating, and very much aware she could still back out. The last thing she wanted was to get involved in some kind of messed-up triangle. The power struggle of two people fighting over their child had to be the worst.

"Nicki, listen to me. If you do this, everyone gets what they want."

She stared at him, unable to determine whether he was telling the truth or not.

"I promise you. It's the best for everyone. Most of all Maddy," he said. "My wife hasn't paid fifteen minutes of attention to her since she got custody—and she only got that because she lived with my in-laws. They passed away last year, within months of each other, and Maddy hasn't been cared for properly since. My ex only keeps her around because of the child support, because it gives her a little more leverage to my bank account."

It occurred to Nicki he was probably being honest about that. Residents jokingly claimed the Gillettes owned half of Winter Park.

"I'm doing this for Maddy's best interests," Jared went on. "My ex suddenly decided she wants to get married—in some cheesy little Las Vegas chapel—and she doesn't want Maddy hanging around."

Nicki blanched, knowing too well how a child could so easily be dismissed.

"I want her," he continued. "She's my daughter, and I can provide for her."

War waged inside Nicki's head. If she had been a vindictive person she'd say no and leave him to his own devices. Yet she'd seen enough on that ten-foot strip of mantel to know he was being sincere. She'd seen Maddy's photos, carefully arranged like a shrine. The Gillette family did appear to be committed to each other, and she did appear to be a lovely child....

"Even you'll get what you want," he said softly. "You'll get the job, the money, everything and anything you could want. I'll see to it."

There really wasn't a choice, and Nicki knew it. She needed the job, she needed the security. Yet, it wasn't just that...she needed a home for Christmas, and he was offering it to her. She'd be a fool to not accept.

"I only need a fair salary," she said shakily. "That's all."

"Done."

Nicki's eyes slid closed, and she wondered if she was making a pact with the devil or Scrooge. "Okay. I have a black sheath in my closet," she said finally, her voice barely above a whisper. "It's nothing special, but it's..." She shrugged somewhat helplessly as she tried to pull off one more lame joke. "Well, it's nicer than the Santa suit. I think it'll do."

Her mother loved glitzy costume jewelry and Nicki hurriedly chose the best pieces—baguette-cut earrings and a matching necklace. Jared didn't seem to notice they were fake, but when she walked out, his eyes widened at the revealing slit in her slim skirt.

"You're right," he said evenly, "this is definitely better than red velvet and fake fur."

Realizing that for the first time he saw her as a woman, not as an employee, not as a baby-sitter, a wave of self-consciousness washed over Nicki. She picked at a piece of nonexistent lint. "The fashion experts claim you can never go wrong with basic black."

"Right. It's simple. Subtle. Sexy..."

She offered him a sharp look, but his face was unreadable. "I don't have a coat," she said, "And my mother's things are three sizes too small, so I thought..." She lifted up a fringed black wool shawl. "Will this be okay? I don't want to embarrass you."

"It's fine."

Taking a deep breath, she expertly draped the shawl around her shoulders, letting it cascade down her arm.

His gaze went dark, heavy-lidded. He abruptly turned away, as if he were already bored with her game of dress-up. "It's a nice condo. I suppose you hate to give it up."

While she put her wallet, keys, a few tissues, and a lipstick into her black clutch, she glanced around the sparsely decorated room. She'd always thought the upscale town house had been too modern. "No. It was my mom's choice. She liked the location."

He nodded. "I noticed this photo, here on the table. Your mom?"

Nicki hesitated uncomfortably, she didn't want to go into it now. She didn't want to explain heart failure to a virile man who most likely only took gasping, self-inflicted breaths when he ran five miles. "Yes," she said, "but...I'm in the process of settling my mom's estate." *Estate? What estate? There'd been nothing left after the medical bills and funeral expenses carved huge chunks out of her life insurance and pension.*

"Oh, I'm sorry. I didn't realize. I just assumed..." To his credit, Jared didn't press for more information, but deftly changed the subject. "You ready to make your debut?"

She nodded, and followed him out the door. He stopped on the steps and offered up his arm. "I don't want you to slip," he said, indicating her strappy shoes.

Nicki hesitated, then reluctantly linked her arm through his. Jared, she immediately learned, was rock-solid. This close, he smelled like designer aftershave and preppie wool blazers. It bothered her, to have that kind of intimate knowledge about him.

The ride to the Ritz Carlton was inordinately quiet. Jared, she guessed, had his mind on his ex-wife. He was probably thinking of everything he needed to do before his daughter arrived. He was probably thinking of lawyers, and old memories, and how his life would change.

"Remember," Jared advised as he pulled into valet parking at the Ritz Carlton, "play it cool. If anyone asks, say we've known each other 'awhile' and leave it at that. We're just making an appearance, really, and that's all we need to do. Just so the rumors circulate and we convince Sandra this is legitimate."

The slit in her dress gaped when Nicki reached for her clutch. Jared's gaze briefly strayed, and she immediately

pinched the folds shut, pinning them with her hand. As if
he had scorched her with his look, Nicki's thigh tingled
with heat.

One valet opened Nicki's door, and Jared accepted a
valet check from another. He came around the corner to
escort Nicki inside as a doorman held open the door. The
ballroom lighting was subdued, yet Nicki couldn't help but
feel as if the air had been charged with electricity once they
entered the room. They followed the maître d' to their assigned seating at one of the front tables, with Jared pausing
to glad-hand every Winter Park businessman and socialite
along the way.

Nicki, acutely conscious of the curious looks, did her best
to nod and smile.

At the table, Jared made cursory introductions.

"And do you work, Nicki?" Janice, the young wife of
the president of Winter Park's largest bank, asked.

The question wanted to make Nicki laugh out loud. The
fact was, she'd had this woman's children sitting on her lap
just last week. Mindy, four, and Michael, five.

"Not right now," Jared smoothly intervened. "She's going to spend Christmas with me. We decided to dress up
the holidays and enjoy them this year."

"You?" her husband boomed. "I know you. You won't
have time to enjoy them, you'll be scrapping for every retail
dollar those customers spend."

"And why are you complaining?" Jared good-naturedly
shot back. "I put it all in your bank."

Everyone at the table laughed. Nicki found she genuinely
enjoyed the company. More interesting, she discovered that
they respected Jared.

When the server placed a filet mignon in front of her,
Nicki stared at it hungrily. It had been a long twelve hours
since she'd breakfasted on a dry bagel and cream cheese—
and so much had happened in between. She'd started out
the day by pulling on a red Santa suit and now she was
dining with the department store president. Incredible. Life

had a way of sneaking up on you when you least expected it.

She shook her head, ravenously surveying the gourmet delight on her plate.

Jared leaned into her, his appearance solicitous. "Everything okay?" he asked.

"Oh, I..." She looked up at him, and their gazes caught and held. Her heart started thrumming. "I was just wondering how I got here."

A smile played over his lips, and his eyes were dark, mysterious, as he leaned even closer. She knew, vaguely, that he was creating an illusion for those at the table, but for a moment she didn't really care. It was so delicious to be a part of something, to have someone appear to care. It had been a long time since someone had taken care of her, or even been concerned about her. She had been lonely for so long.

She basked in the feelings he created, even when he hung his arm across the back of her chair and squeezed her shoulder. Even when she knew it was false.

Two of the women made note of the gesture, she realized, getting a sudden, uncomfortable wallop of reality.

Jared, it seemed, made a show of reluctantly tearing his gaze away and asking the man next to him a question.

Nicki was still eating when the emcee for the gala introduced those responsible and outlined the charities that would benefit from the evening's festivities. She nearly dropped her fork when Jared Gillette was summoned to the podium.

No one seemed to notice, and Nicki politely joined them, clapping while Jared made his way to the platform. She carefully arranged her face, as if she'd known all along this was going to happen.

A beam of light hovered on Jared's shoulders as he stepped through the crowd. His elegant tuxedo hung perfectly, outlining his tall, lithe frame. As he walked up the steps, his solid good looks were profiled, making him appear one notch short of angelic when he turned to the crowd and offered up a dazzling smile.

A shiver went through Nicki.

"On behalf of Gillette's Department Store," he said, "I am pleased to present the Yuletide Gala with a check for twenty-five thousand dollars. This money has been designated to benefit the city respite program for parents of developmentally disabled children as well as caregivers of the ill and recovering. On a personal note, I want to thank every volunteer who so generously gives their time to this remarkable program. Thank you. Your efforts are sincerely appreciated."

A ripple went through the crowd. It had been the largest donation that evening, and thunderous applause echoed through the ballroom.

A hot, searing pain rolled through Nicki's chest, even as she experienced a flicker of pride for Jared's gesture. Those around her clapped wildly, and stood. She followed their example, closely watching Jared's reaction.

He appeared unaffected, nodding as he walked back through the crowd, a firm smile on his lips. Nicki was in awe of how easily he handled the adulation.

He resumed his place by her, and waved to the crowd. Then he did the most unexpected thing—he reached over for her hand and captured it, twining his fingers possessively through hers. Nicki went weak, and her heart pounded. Still claiming her hand, he guided her back into her seat, and nudged his own into place.

"That was impressive," she whispered as everyone resumed their seats.

"I wasn't trying to be impressive," he said drolly, "I was trying to do a little good."

"You did. No coal in your stocking this year."

The corner of his mouth lifted. "Can you guarantee it?"

"Trust me," she said, her voice heavy with innuendo, "I have my connections."

Jared smiled, then accepted a round of congratulations

and thanks at the table. Almost immediately afterward the orchestra began to play and people filtered to the dance floor or to dessert stations at the back of the room.

"Dance?" Jared invited, tossing his napkin onto the table.

"Oh, you don't have to..." Nicki trailed off, not quite sure what his intentions were. Several couples from their table were already dancing, but she knew he didn't want to stay.

His eyes seemed to mock her. "Maybe I want to," he suggested. "Maybe it's good for the illusion. Maybe it's part of what *works* between us," he emphasized.

Nicki stared at him, then reluctantly stood. Okay. If this was part of her job, making a few swings around the dance floor, she'd cooperate.

He stood aside for her to precede him, then reached for her hand as they wove their way through the tables. He led her onto the dance floor as though she were a queen. Nicki lifted her head, knowing all eyes were on her. Inside, her nerve endings quickened and blood pounded in her ears.

They were barely six feet onto the dance floor when he pulled her into his arms. They made a few experimental steps around the floor. She followed his lead perfectly, matching her steps to his, feeling her body intuit his every move.

"Everyone's looking, aren't they?" he asked against her ear.

"Yes," she said, looking over his shoulder and trying to avoid eye contact with all the curious guests.

He pulled her imperceptibly closer, but leaned back from the waist, engaging her in private conversation. His hips intimately ground against hers. "You're absolutely sure everyone's looking?"

Her eyes flickered away. "Y-yes."

"Good." He abruptly spun her in a quick circle, then made a slow, seductive dip to the music. His arm supported her. She looked up into his excruciatingly handsome face, while an overhead disco ball threw a dozen scintillating sparks over his tuxedo. "Now I'm going to kiss you," he said huskily. "Pretend you like it."

Chapter Four

Nicki had little time to react to his warning. Her eyes widened and she opened her mouth, intending to protest. She refused to allow anything so ridiculous! But Jared tugged her tight against him. His face hovered only inches above hers and, with determination etched on his finely chiseled features, he slowly, methodically, lowered his head.

There was no way out.

Nicki closed her eyes, and braced herself to endure the indignity.

As if he could feel her tense, Jared imperceptibly kneaded her back and the flesh at her ribs. "I guarantee this isn't going to hurt," he whispered, his breath soft against her cheek and brow. "Do your best to enjoy it."

Nicki felt her eyelashes flutter, and she wiggled, slightly, in his embrace. Then, as her initial apprehension faded, his lips swooped down, claiming her, and pulling her into a hot, passionate kiss. The world spun out of control and Nicki found herself spiralling into a vortex of need as everything behind her closed eyelids turned blue-black. She felt as fuzzy as velvet, as warm as wool, and she clung to him as he parted her lips and deepened the kiss.

Her lungs ached for want of air; blood pounded and rushed her veins, yammering in her ears, making her feel weak, dizzy.

The kiss was so good that she nearly forgot why she was there and what his intentions were. His palate offered an intoxicating mixture of chocolate, wine and cherries. The combination of chocolate and wine was as seductive as an aphrodisiac; the tangy hint of cherries on his tongue left her craving more.

The kiss became fervent, demanding. Seconds ticked away before he expertly pulled back. Even then, his mouth still teased hers, his nose ending the intimacy with a tempting Eskimo kiss.

Nicki struggled to open her eyes, and a sigh involuntarily rippled through her. Her reflexes tightened as he released her, and she was vaguely conscious that her fingertips were biting the shoulders of his tuxedo.

A low sound of approval rumbled through Jared's chest. Then he chuckled, effortlessly lifting her, his strong arms still twining at her back. "You," he whispered, "are an amazing actress."

Actress? What was he talking about? Nicki thought woozily. Hearing an edge to his voice, she desperately tried to focus. His face floated over hers, and her attention centered on the cleft in his chin, the jutting angle of his jaw. Above, his brow was shadowed, his mud-dark gaze perceptive.

The realization hit her like a dash of cold water. He thought she was trying to seduce *him!*

The scenario, unbidden, rolled through her head: Winter Park's most-sought-after bachelor routinely fought off the advances of every gold digger within a five-hundred-mile radius. He thought she was one of those!

"I—I was only trying to make things look…genuine," she said, leaning back into his supporting hand and trying to put some distance between her chest and his. "At your request."

His gaze bored into hers, but his mouth twitched indulgently. "Yes. Well, it was a convincing performance. I can't fault you for that. Maybe I'll have to give you a bonus."

A feeling of helplessness, even defeat, washed over her. How was she going to work for this man if he second-guessed everything she said, everything she did? And it was insulting, for him to think everything she did was based on money. "Jared, this isn't going to work. I know what you're thinking and—"

He seemed to anticipate her objections before she uttered them. "Shh," he interrupted. "It'll be fine. This is just a one-time thing, and we both know it. So what? I was the one who ordered up the command performance," he admitted, lifting a shoulder. "Don't be so defensive about kissing me back."

He had picked up the beat of the music and they were dancing again, smoothly and without a hint of hesitation. Nicki had followed his lead, and hadn't even realized it. "I wasn't kissing you back," she hissed, talking into his shoulder so no one could see or make out what they were saying to each other.

"Really? So you didn't enjoy it?"

A cold, hard feeling settled in the pit of Nicki's stomach. She never had been good at bold, outright lies. Stretching the truth a little, like playing the part of Santa Claus or filling in as Jared's current love interest, was entirely different. "Keep in mind," she said finally, "that I'm only doing my job."

"And let me just say, my little *Saint Nicholas,* that you do it very well."

Amusement flickered behind Jared's eyes, and for an instant Nicki wondered if he was baiting her. She'd never admit that his kiss had left her shaken. If anything, he'd simply caught her off guard...because she certainly wasn't attracted to him. She liked good, solid men. Men who worked hard, played hard, and were committed to a strict set of values. Jared Gillette had been born with a silver spoon in his mouth—he had no idea what the real world was about. He had no idea what it felt like to hurt.

It was seven o'clock on a Sunday morning and Nicki lay in her bed, awake, and staring at the ceiling. With the back of her wrist, she rubbed her mouth, remembering the kiss she'd shared with Jared. What had she done? What had she gotten herself into?

At the time it had seemed so innocent, even silly. She had gone along with his hare-brained kissing idea, only because she didn't want to argue. Not there, not in front of a hundred curious onlookers. She had never anticipated her reaction—not in a million years. She'd expected a chaste, affectionate kiss and wound up experiencing an intimacy so profound it had left her shaken.

Of course, it was all a mistake. He'd upended her hormones with his brusque manner and kind ways—it was a deadly combination, that was all there was to it. A business deal that had gone over the edge because they'd mixed in a little pleasure.

Last night, they'd left soon after their fateful dance, and he'd dropped her off at her mother's condo with strict instructions to be ready because he'd pick her up at 8:00 a.m. today. He wanted to discuss the game plan for bringing Madison into his home. Nicki fully expected that when he arrived he'd be the tyrant she'd met yesterday.

In a way, she regretted it. He *had* been nice during dinner last night, if only for a little while.

Snagging a deep breath, Nicki swung her legs over the side of the bed, and reminded herself she didn't have a choice. It didn't matter who she was dealing with—the tyrant or the tolerable family man—she needed the job.

Jared Gillette was five minutes early. Nicki opened the door with one hand and finished buttoning her blouse with the other. It was an action she regretted, particularly when Jared's assessing gaze raked her front.

"Come in," she invited, purposely ignoring his automated male response system. "I made coffee. Can I get you some?"

"Actually, I..." Jared frowned, and trailed a look over her bare feet. "I thought we'd go to my place, but I can see you aren't ready."

Nicki wiggled her toes. Flirtatiously. Each toenail, painted cranberry-red, rippled over the plush green carpet. What in the world had gotten into her? Had her subconscious found some kind of perverse way to goad the man? "I just need to put my shoes on," she apologized needlessly. "I know you said eight o'clock, but I guess I thought we'd be staying here to talk."

He nodded, grimly, as if he were a man with a purpose, a man in a hurry. "I wanted you to look over Madison's room, as well as yours. I expect we'll have to make some appropriate changes, and I want to discuss your duties."

Nicki padded into the kitchen to unplug the coffeepot and grab her shoes.

Without invitation, Jared followed. "That coffee does smell good," he allowed, his gaze straying to the half-filled carafe.

At the counter Nicki swiveled and automatically reached for a coffee cup. What the heck? She wouldn't make him ask. She could have given him a dishwasher-safe mug, but chose instead one of her mother's bone china favorites. As she filled it, she figured it would serve as an introduction: *Jared Gillette, meet my soft-spoken, kind-hearted mother.*

She offered the cup to him, quickly moving her fingers out of the way so they'd never have the opportunity to touch. She glanced up at him then, and realized his attention was not on the fine china. His eyes drifted over her mouth, lazily, as if he were considering the intimate kiss they had shared last night.

Nicki immediately turned away. She pulled out a kitchen

chair and yanked on her socks before stepping into her tennis shoes. She didn't want to second-guess Jared Gillette, or his kisses. Yet, from the corner of her eye, she kept track of him as she brought an ankle to her opposite knee to tighten her shoelace.

He leaned against her counter, sipping the coffee. "Good coffee," he remarked, but his gaze slid down the curve of her jeans. Finally tearing his eyes away, he looked over the cup, to the opposite wall, to the framed family photos. "Is that you?"

"Mmm, yes. That's the life event thing. Mom and her little girl." Nicki was acutely aware there was no father in any of the snapshots that chronicled her life; she wondered if Jared would notice. She was six when her father had walked out on them. Shortly thereafter, all photos of him had mysteriously disappeared—just like her father.

Nicki tied her shoes and stood, pulling on a sweater before she grabbed her light blue jacket.

Seeing that she was ready, Jared frowned, then downed his coffee.

He escorted her outside in record time. Nicki paused on the steps, looking for his Lincoln. He gestured to a dark green Corvette. "I thought I'd drive something more casual today."

"Oh. Nice. A car wardrobe." Nicki wanted to bite her tongue off. The man couldn't help it if he wallowed in money. "I'm sorry. I didn't mean to make that sound like—"

"Don't apologize. There are days the Lincoln makes me feel stodgy. This is one of them."

She took in Jared's leather jacket, his sweater and slacks, knowing he was anything but stodgy. He opened her car door and Nicki slid into the bucket seat.

They drove for several minutes in silence. "You're quiet this morning," he finally said. "You aren't thinking of backing out of our arrangement, are you?"

An uneasy feeling prickled over Nicki's scalp. The fact

was, she'd considered it more times than she wanted to count. She fiddled with the strap on her watch, using the moment to avoid a direct answer. "I didn't get a lot of sleep last night, that's all."

He shot her a questioning look.

"Hey," she explained, lifting both shoulders, "a lot happened in the past twenty-four hours. I got fired from a job, got hired for a job. I saw you at work, and at home. I felt like Cinderella standing on the street corner, and then later like the belle of the ball at the Yuletide Gala." Nicki intentionally avoided any reminders that she posed as his girlfriend—or the ill-fated kiss they'd shared. "All in all, it was a little bit much and it left me with a lot to think about."

He turned onto Lyman Avenue, the Corvette wheeling the corner. "Last night's kiss didn't have anything to do with your lack of sleep, did it?"

Nicki stiffened. "Of course not. My mind was on something entirely different." She went on, "I never planned on staying in Winter Park. I kept thinking about how staying could affect my plans."

"Oh. Really?" He didn't sound convinced.

"My mom moved here a couple of years ago, to take a receptionist job, but then her health started failing. I came back to take care of her, and I figured when the lease was up, I'd close up the condo and move back to Florida. Then the car became an issue, and—"

"I know. We've got to do something about that," he interrupted. "I expect you to have transportation." A second slipped away. "It never occurred to me. You *can* drive, can't you?"

"Of course I can drive," she said indignantly, pulling back, convinced he hadn't heard a word she'd said about her mom or why she was here or anything.

"I mean, can you drive well? Because if Maddy's going to be with you—"

"My car died, I didn't kill it," she stated emphatically.

"I don't have a glove box full of speeding tickets, and I've never been in accident. But the car's twelve years old, and I'm just not sure whether to fix it or junk it. It needs a new alternator, new shocks, brakes, tires, and—"

"That bad?"

"According to the mechanic."

"Junk it," he said decisively. "I'll make arrangements for you to drive my SUV. That'll be the safest for you and Madison anyway."

Nicki was momentarily stunned into silence. "Do you…collect cars or something?"

"No, I just believe everything has a purpose."

"Yeah," she agreed dryly, "this Corvette really serves a purpose."

He snorted. "It's my hurry-up car."

"Your hurry-up car," she repeated.

"My hurry-up-and-live-a-little car," he informed her. "And today I feel like I've been given a license to live a little, now that I'm getting my daughter back."

He meant what he said; Nicki knew that. Still, as he turned into gated drive of his home, she tried to picture what kind of father he would be. Would he keep his daughter at arm's length, dismissing her to Nicki and forgetting she even existed? Or, would he be constantly looking over Nicki's shoulder, criticizing her, and lambasting her for any indiscretion?

Either option was a daunting possibility, especially for someone who had lived the life Nicki had.

The estate looked different in the early morning light: quiet, sedate, and perfectly manicured. Nicki guessed Madison's arrival would certainly take the edge off the old-money look of affluence and station. Still, she couldn't imagine a youngster doing cartwheels on the front lawn, or blowing bubbles on the front steps. She couldn't conceive of shrieks and giggles echoing from one end of the family room to the other, not when Jared came home with a headache and a briefcase of troubles.

He'd be impatient and surly, and they'd all run for cover.

Oh, brother. Her imagination might be in overdrive, but common sense told her this job could be even more short-lived than the last one.

"Come on. I want to show you Madison's room," Jared said, easing the Corvette into park.

Nicki followed him in the back door, and through the family room. Little had changed from the previous night, except that she noted the jacket of his tuxedo was carelessly tossed over the arm of the couch. An irresistible vision of Jared, his wide shoulders and lean length highlighted by satin lapels and black-button studs, flitted through her mind.

She followed him into the center hall, then stopped short. The foyer was grand, with a brilliant chandelier that dropped down into a circular cavity created by the winding, oak staircase. Jared's heels clipped across the black marble floor.

"Living room's in there," he indicated. "And the dining room, my office, and the library's beyond." He headed up the stairs, ahead of her. "Madison's room really hasn't been touched since Sandra moved out. The crib's still up, and her toys are still on the shelves. I'll need you to use your best judgment in what goes and what stays. I can arrange for someone to pack everything up for you and remove it. But I want it done as quickly as possible."

Nicki took a deep breath, suddenly wary of making these decisions. "Don't you want to oversee some of this? Maybe you have some special things you'd like to keep, for her, or yourself, or—"

He paused on the landing and turned toward her, his eyes one shade darker than she remembered. "I got up early this morning and took care of that. From here out, use your own discretion. This is a new start, and I want to make sure she falls in love with this room. You can get new furniture, and anything you need. But, most of all, I want to make sure that she feels safe and secure, like she's finally come home again.''

"Okay," she said carefully. "I'll do my best."

He moved down the hall, then reached across her to the last door and pushed it open. Nicki caught her breath. Mullioned-glass windows opened onto a balcony that overlooked the back lawn. The room, hopelessly romantic, and done in ivory and white, had gentle touches of peach and blue pastels. Overhead, above the crown molding, the arched ceiling was a swirl of wispy clouds and chubby cherubs.

It was every woman's dream, to have a nursery like this for her firstborn. It pulled at her heartstrings, to think of cradling a baby in this magical, whimsical room.

Nicki slowly stepped inside, pensively trailing a hand over the arm of a rocker. Her attention shifted from the shelves of books and toddler pull-toys to the play table and tiny chairs. "Oh, my. This is incredible. Absolutely incredible." She twirled in the middle of the room, taking in all the details. "I can't believe you want to dismantle this room," she said. "It's too wonderful."

Jared leaned against the door frame. "That part of my life is over," he said curtly. "This is the only room in the entire house Sandra and I redecorated—and it's a nursery. For babies and their mothers. I won't have any more children passing through it, because I have no intention—and certainly no inclination—of having more children. I'm not ever making the mistake of marrying again."

Nicki's heart inexplicably clenched, and she stopped moving. Something seemed so wrong, so final, about his declaration.

"The bottom line is that Madison's outgrown this room," he went on. "Time to throw out the old and move on with the new. Do whatever you have to do. Just don't bother me about it."

Nicki glanced over her shoulder at him, sharply, sensing his flip replies were a cover. For what? she asked herself.

Regrets? Pain? Guilt? Over a marriage that didn't work out?
Or a sense of loss over the father he'd never been?

She looked back up at the ceiling. "Can I at least save
the ceiling?" she asked, simultaneously trying to strike both
the awe and the pleas from her voice. "It's so beautiful. I
feel like I've been transported to some European chapel."

Jared lifted a noncommittal shoulder, and his eyes hard-
ened. "Suit yourself."

"I mean...you don't want me to redo this room with
cartoon characters and bunk beds, do you? You don't want
posters and a black light?"

He choked and a reluctant smile pursed his lips. "It just
needs to be different, is all, something a child would enjoy.
I want Madison to want to stay."

Nicki nodded, and beat back the urge to pull the string
on the yellow duck to watch him wobble and quack. She
longed to nudge the tiny cradle, too, where a dolly, dressed
in a frilly white gown and bonnet, was propped against a
lacy pillow. She imagined sitting back in the rocker, a
youngster on her lap, as she savored the beautifully illus-
trated children's books.

"My room is across the hall, on the front of the house,"
Jared said, interrupting her thoughts. "The family always
preferred this wing because it was quieter."

"It's a lovely home," Nicki said. *Mansion,* she silently
revised. "I suppose you grew up here?"

"For the most part," Jared replied. "Your room's at the
other end of the other wing. I apologize for it being so far
away, but I figured you'd need the largest suite." He moved
out of the doorway and started down the hall, obviously
expecting her to follow.

Nicki took one last, lingering look at the magnificent
nursery, then hurried after him. "Thank you, but I don't
need anything that fancy, or that large. Just an ordinary
room will do."

"No, it's already settled," he said, never breaking stride.
"Look it over. If you think of anything you need, let me

know. Or if you think you're going to have trouble getting your belongings to fit, we can arrange for storage, or—''

Nicki caught up with him, and waved away the suggestion. "No. It'll be fine. I travel light."

His eyes flickered, as if he were filing away the bit of information. "There were some nice pieces of furniture in your condo. I thought—''

"No. Nothing of sentimental value," she said quickly, knowing she couldn't very well explain that after her dad left them they'd lost the house, and taken a small apartment, eventually putting all their extra things in storage. Later, everything in it had gone to the highest bidder when her mom had failed to make the payments on the storage unit. Her childhood memories had been carted away in cardboard boxes, by folks who relished the bargains of a single mother's misfortune. It had been a cruel lesson in "only the strong survive."

He paused, his hand settling over the doorknob of a closed door. "I think you'll be comfortable here," he said, pushing the door open. Nicki stepped inside. "My mom had these rooms refurbished after she lost my dad, hoping all her friends would come and visit. It's *not,*" he emphasized, "the maid's quarters."

Nicki bit her lower lip, trying not to smile. This room, as his probably did, faced the front. The view from the windows was parklike. Evergreens and shade trees and statuary lined the huge expanse of lawn and circular front drive, with the wrought-iron fencing separating the estate from the street and boulevard.

"There's an efficiency kitchen in here." Jared slid open a paneled pocket door, calling her attention away. "A turnaround, really. Good enough for breakfasts and a midnight snack, I suppose."

Nicki gaped at the small, state-of-the-art refrigerator, sink, dishwasher, espresso machine and microwave. "It's all I'll need," she stated.

"Well, I'll expect you to eat your meals with Madison.

Use the kitchen downstairs whenever you want, but I'll warn you, the kitchen is my housekeeper's domain and she's protective of it. If you make a mess, you'll answer to her. I won't run interference for you.''

Nicki nodded. "Thanks, I'll remember that," she said, backing from the doorway. There was a luxurious bath next to the tiny kitchen, and a huge sitting area separate from the bedroom. "This is lovely," she remarked, taking in the damask-covered chairs, the cherrywood coffee tables, and gilt-edged mirrors.

"Lovely, but I have a feeling it's not your style," he remarked pointedly.

It wasn't. Not at all. Nicki preferred warm oak and the comfort of country styling to this kind of elegance. "It's more than I need," she said honestly, "and far more than I expected."

"The offer stands. You can bring in whatever you want."

"Thank you." It was an offer easy enough to accept because Nicki knew she wasn't bringing any more than the bare necessities from the condo and she wasn't going to be here long enough to object to anything. This was one more transition in her life. She needed the money, the change of pace, and the sense of family. As she eased out of her old life, it would be a diversion to ease Jared into his new one. Maybe, for just a little while, she could feel as though she belonged.

"I'm going to the store early today," he announced, breaking into her thoughts. "And I want you to go with me. Look things over. I expect you to start making decisions on everything from Christmas presents for Madison, to sheets and towels for her room. I'll arrange for you to have carte blanche to pick out whatever you need." His gaze lingered on her blue jacket. "Is that understood?"

"Yes. But if you don't like my choices—"

"I won't hesitate to tell you."

"Do you have any suggestions, or—"

"Something that would please a child. I don't want to be bothered with the details."

Nicki swallowed and, lifting both eyebrows, turned away so he couldn't see her roll her eyes. Then she looked across the room, and their eyes collided via the gilt-edged mirror. She wanted to just die. She was mortified he'd caught her mocking him, and a guilty flush crept up the back of her neck.

"And while you're doing those things," he said crossly, "get yourself a real winter coat. I get cold just looking at you."

Chapter Five

"Buy myself a coat?" Nicki asked, unable to strike the disbelief from her voice. The offer—or was it criticism?—tumbled through her head. She couldn't decide if Jared was being generous or scathing. There was a certain indignity about accepting warm clothing from someone you barely knew, particularly if that someone was your employer.

"Yes, and put it on my bill."

"I couldn't. Not possibly. I can afford my own things...I just haven't had time to find something that—" *Liar.*

"Consider it an incentive. You and your cheeky behavior have already earned it," he said, ushering her out into the hall and closing the door to the suite. "Come on, let's get going. I get ten times more done when no one's at the store."

Nicki, figuring she deserved the cheeky behavior comment, trailed after him, then hurried to catch up. "Jared, about the coat? Forget it. I don't expect you to provide me with things like that. I'll work on my wardrobe. I'm sure you want me to look appropriate, because you probably have a lot of people coming through the house, and—"

He whirled impatiently, pivoting on the heel of his shoe. For an instant Nicki's resolve plummeted and she was half afraid she'd angered him.

"What?" he asked incredulously, his eyes locking with hers. "You think that is what this is all about?" He shook his head. "No. It's not about appearances. There's absolutely nothing wrong with the way you look. Nothing," he repeated. "But I'm trying to do you, and myself, too, a favor. I don't ever want to see you shivering and shaking from the cold like you were last night. It was outrageous, and I won't have it."

"But…" The word died on her lips.

His features softened, slightly, as if he had second thoughts about the orders he was tossing around. "It's a small thing, Nicki. Really. Especially when I consider all you'll be doing for me." A smile played at his lips. "Come on. You didn't have any trouble wearing the red velvet and fake fur I provided you with."

"That was different."

"No different than me paying you to do a job. This job."

Nicki could feel herself giving in. He owed it to her, really. After all he'd put her through: the angst, the indecision, the uncertainties. "As for the job," she said carefully, "I still don't know enough about it. Not about you. Or about Madison."

He leaned back, slightly, his eyelids dropping to half mast as if he were measuring her response. He knew, already, that he'd won the issue with the coat. "We're going to be spending a lot of time together the next few days. I imagine you'll find out more about me—and Madison— than you really want to know."

He made it sound ominous, as if she'd be disappointed by what she discovered. "There are things I know about you I already like," she said softly. "The way you donated money to the respite program—"

"Why would you care about that?" he asked.

She paused. "I had to take care of my mom when she

was sick. There were days I would have traded my soul for two hours' worth of sleep or a hot meal. It was the respite program that came in and helped out in ways I could never have imagined. I'll be forever in their debt.''

Jared looked startled, as if he had no idea his gesture had the capability of genuinely affecting someone's life. "I—I didn't know," he said uncomfortably.

"I probably should have told you last night," Nicki admitted. "But I don't talk about it much. Families belong together, especially during the holidays, and this year I've had my moments when I've felt kind of overwhelmed— like it's just too hard to go it alone, and get through Christmas. I suppose this first year without my mom will be the worst." Jared's gaze became veiled, his mouth curling suspiciously. "I'm not saying that to make you feel guilty about yesterday, or the Santa Claus job or anything," she said hastily. "You couldn't have known."

"You have to understand something, Nicki...I never feel guilty about business. No matter how personal it becomes."

Nicki refused to be swayed. Taking his words with a grain of salt, she smiled shyly up at him, hoping he didn't rebuff the intimacy she chose to share. "Even so, seeing how eager you are to get your daughter back—especially at Christmas—kind of warms me a little. It's even better than a winter coat, Jared. Don't worry about me, I'll get along."

His jaw went hard. "Look here, St. Nick. Don't go all sappy on me, because it's not going to fly. Just thank me— or better yet, thank Gillette's Department Store for the coat, and we'll call it even. I don't do well with warm fuzzies, so you're wasting them on me."

He started to move away, but Nicki laid a hand on his arm, stopping him. Her steady gaze had the strangest effect: it made his eyes flicker with surprise. "Thank you, Jared," she whispered. "For everything."

Jared Gillette, Nicki soon learned, did not want to be known for being nice. He was honest, forthright, and just, but he didn't dole out kind words and he didn't expect to be rewarded or recognized for any tidbit of generosity. He listened to anything Nicki said about her personal life, but he was hard-pressed to share information on his own.

Nicki thought about that the entire time she shopped Gillette's Department Store. She'd spent the day wandering from one display to another. She was bone-tired and weary, her feet ached and her head throbbed. It was doubly hard making decisions for others, but for people you didn't even know it was downright impossible.

She picked out colors she guessed would complement the ceiling mural—muted teal and soft-shell coral—all the while considering the man behind the facade. Any man who loved his child as much as Jared obviously did, could not be all grinch or grouch. Still, he kept himself and his feelings in close check, keeping everyone and everything at arm's distance. It was as if every time he felt her getting close, he pushed her away.

Maybe it was the divorce, maybe it was his position, his social standing. Or, maybe it was just who he was. But with the barriers he kept throwing up, Nicki knew it would be difficult to work with him on a daily basis. There was only one thing to do, she vowed. Tear the walls down and uncover the heart of the man beneath.

At fifteen minutes to closing, Nicki asked a clerk in the Home Shoppe to bag two prints, and set off to find Jared.

She popped into the department store offices, which were again empty. Timidly knocking at the forbidding mahogany door, she experienced a bit of déjà vu. This was too much like yesterday, she thought insanely. Here she was, doing it again, expecting the same chilly invitation.

"Come in," Jared barked.

Carefully easing open the door, Nicki peeked inside his office. "I'm sorry to interrupt, but I need your opinion."

Jared frowned, then pulled the phone away from his ear, and motioned to her to sit while he finished his conversation. "I want that truck unloaded, and I don't care if those guys on the dock have to work overtime to do it." He listened impatiently. "So? Christmas comes but once a year, and when it comes, we at Gillette's pounce on it. They get overtime anyway, so what are they griping about?" He dropped the phone in the cradle and looked, pointedly, at Nicki. "Yes?"

"I see you've got problems, and I *am* sorry to intrude," she apologized.

"Problems? What problems?"

"Well, you..." She indicated the phone. "I thought..."

"That's not a problem. It's routine everyday business." He half sighed, half laughed. "Now...what is it you want?"

"An opinion. Yours, please." She pulled the Raggedy Ann print out of the shopping bag. "What do you think?"

"Nice."

She hesitated. His ambivalent reaction was not very encouraging. She pulled a second print from the bag. "What about this?"

He impatiently stared at the print of cherubs wrapped in trailing sheets of oatmeal-colored cloth and running through a meadow filled with flowers. "It's..." He lifted a shoulder, shaking his head. "Okay, I guess."

Deflation oozed through Nicki, and she looked back at the print. "It's my favorite," she said. "It would be so beautiful with the ceiling. And they have prints with cherubs on a seesaw, and a swing, and one where they dance with rose petals falling like rain. They're so beautiful, but..."

"Would you like to tell me why you're bothering me with this?"

"Because I was afraid it might be the kind of print only adults can appreciate. I don't even know Madison. But she would probably like dolls or cartoon characters or—"

"Who knows? She probably won't even care."

Nicki couldn't bring herself to leave his office, she knew she was pushing, but she wanted his approval. "They're just so inspirational. So dear. They're in muted colors and there're eight or ten different prints." Nicki ran a fingertip along the edge of the antique-finished frame. "Don't they just touch your heart and make you go soft all over?"

Jared arched an eyebrow, as if he couldn't believe he'd heard her correctly. He drummed his fingertips over a sheaf of papers. "No. They don't."

Nicki tried to backpedal. "I know they'll look wonderful in the room. But what I don't know is if Madison will like them, that's the thing."

Jared leaned back in his chair, and pushed the file out of the way. "I've only got a few minutes to closing, St. Nick. Go down to the Home Shoppe and wait for me there. But while you're waiting, get the prints you want. No. Get all the prints. We'll take them home and try them."

Nicki couldn't help herself; she broke into a wide smile. "Thanks," she said. "I think you're really going to like them."

"Whatever," he replied, flapping a hand in her direction.

Knowing she'd been dismissed, Nicki picked up the bags and rose, starting for the door.

"By the way," he said, his voice at her back, "did you get the coat?"

With her hand still on the doorknob, she turned to face him, nodding. "I did. It's warm, serviceable, and perfect for—"

"'Serviceable'?"

"Well, yes, it's a nice sturdy coat."

"Nice and sturdy as in—" he lifted a shoulder "—say, practical?"

"It will be very practical, especially for taking Madison around, running in and out. It's got a hood, deep pockets. It buttons, it zips, it's rain repellent—"

"Mmm-hmm. That's what I was afraid of." He slammed shut a drawer, and came around the desk. "It's probably got a zip-out lining, too."

Nicki had the strangest feeling that she shouldn't admit that it did. "Well..." The word twisted on her tongue.

"Okay," he announced. "That's it. I'm done for the day." He grabbed his leather coat off the coat tree. "After we do this print thing, we do the coat thing. I don't want you wandering around looking like somebody's grand-mother."

He strode over to the door.

"Wait a minute," she said, unconsciously laying a hand on his chest to stop him. A tingle went through her finger-tips, momentarily distracting her. "I thought you were the one who wasn't concerned about appearances. That's what you said this morning. I was just trying to do the right thing, by you, and for your family, and..."

They stood there for the longest moment. He stared down at her, his eyes unreadable depths. Finally he raised his arm and covered the back of her hand with his, gently removing it. His fingers slipped inside her palm and for another brief second they stood there, holding hands in the most awkward manner, and gazing into each other's eyes.

He loosened her hand. "This isn't about appearances," he said huskily. "Not at all. This is about you having too much pride to accept my gift."

Disbelief rippled through her. Funny. Her mother had always said she had too much pride. She'd never liked to ask for help. After her dad left, she'd assumed an I'll-do-it-myself-or-do-without attitude.

"I'm not trying to take advantage of you, Jared. It seems to me you must have a lot of people expecting things, hang-ing their hand out, and I—"

He laughed mirthlessly. "How did you know about my ex-wife?"

In spite of her discomfort, she offered him a thin smile. "I didn't. I can only assume, that by your life, and the way you live, you must have days when you wonder who your friends are. I know that my working for you is just a job. This is temporary, and someday it will be over. By the time

I walk away, I guarantee that you'll have gotten your
money's worth out of that coat, and to me that is what your
'gift' was all about. It will serve the purpose, and that's
how I made my decision.''

"Really?"

Nicki nodded.

"Well, guess what? The boss is overriding your decision.''

The prints, all ten of them, were carefully packaged and
sitting on the plush divan in the women's department. The
store was empty, and the lighting dim. Nicki had seen one
security guard crane his head around the clothing racks just
long enough to see Jared push two wool coats at her. The
expression on his face was incredulous; he obviously
couldn't believe Jared Gillette was fussing over a woman's
coat in his own department store.

"That jacket looks like a lumpy sack of potatoes,'' Jared
groused.

Nicki jammed both hands into the brown canvas pockets
and stared at her reflection in the mirror. "You sell it,'' she
pointed out defensively.

"Yes. My mistake. Remind me to speak to my buyers.''
He looked from one to the other of the coats he'd chosen,
then offered her the cobalt-blue wool one first. She could
only guess at the price tag.

"That's awfully expensive,'' she warned. "And it will
have to be dry cleaned.''

He glanced at the other coat. Red wool, black piping,
with slash pockets and huge round buttons. "Fine. We'll
take them both, so you'll have a spare when one's at the
cleaner's. Of course, it will make a mess of my inventory,
not to be able to put them on my account yet tonight, so
that's an inconvenience. Remind me to do that tomorrow,
too.''

"Jared—''

He didn't budge, but just extended the blue coat to her.

Nicki sighed, and reluctantly slid out of the fat canvas jacket. She hung it back on the hangar and put it aside. When she turned back, Jared was standing patiently with the coat open, to help her slip her arms into the sleeves.

Nicki self-consciously put her back to him to allow him the courtesy.

She could actually feel her cheeks flush when he eased the garment up and over her shoulders. His hands, warm and heavy, lingered at the back of her neck, adjusting the collar, smoothing the shoulder seams. A prickle went over her scalp as he hooked a lock of her hair, dragging it up and splaying it over the collar. Inside the coat, she felt hot and jittery.

Jared's fingers curled over the caps of her sleeves, gently squeezing. "Very nice," he said approvingly.

For want of something to do, Nicki buttoned the double-breasted front and tried the pockets. When she looked up, their gazes caught in the mirror. As they had earlier that morning.

Uncertainty roiled through Nicki's middle. She couldn't do this. He was making her feel all quivery inside. As though his male hormones had dulled her to the fact he was her employer. *Her employer.* It was one thing to have something warm to wear, it was quite another to feel this extraordinary amount of attraction for the man you work for.

"It's too much," she started to protest.

"Did I tell you," he said smoothly, averting his eyes and brushing at a nonexistent piece of lint on the back of the coat, "that I heard from my ex-wife this afternoon?"

Nicki's eyes widened. For the life of her she couldn't imagine what he intended to say, or even why he'd say it. He was tempting her with intimate knowledge about himself, his life—and for a split second Nicki fought the urge to run. She didn't want to know anything intimate about him; he did maddening things to her senses, he made her feel strong and weak at the same time. Hot and cold at the most inopportune moments.

"Remember how I told you she'd have her little runners check you out last night at the gala?" he went on.

"Yes..." Nicki's voice quavered.

"Well, she did. Just as I predicted. Seems like you got their unanimous approval. She said she'll let Madison stay indefinitely. You made a good impression, Nicki, and she feels like, from what she's heard, you might be good for Madison."

"Jared...I was only doing what you asked me to."

"But you did it well," he said. "Maybe my ex doesn't want the responsibility, but she does want the best for Madison. In her heart, she knows that Madison would have a better life with me. Not long ago, she put Madison in the middle, holding her hostage, and rarely letting me see her." He expelled a weary breath, his hold turning viselike on her shoulders. "I don't think I've pieced together a whole week alone with that child since Sandra took her to California. She always had an excuse why my visits wouldn't work into their schedule."

Witnessing his anguish, pity washed through Nicki. "I'm sorry, Jared. Truly."

"Yes, well..." His hands slid from her coat sleeves, and he backed away. "It hasn't been for lack of trying on my part. I thought I should tell you that I haven't seen Madison since last summer. She barely knows me. And God knows what Sandra's told her. Sometimes, when I talk to her on the phone, she doesn't..." His jaw clenched.

"It's going to be an adjustment, and I understand that." She half turned to face him. "But time has an incredible way of—"

"Forget that," he snorted. "Forget the sentimental thoughts. All time did was steal her away from me. What I don't know is why the hell I'm trying to explain this to you anyway," he said harshly. Nicki stiffened, recoiling from his intensity. "I never talk about this. Never."

After Nicki pulled herself together, the revelation went

through her like a flash. Jared wasn't trying to shut her out of his life, he was trying to block out the pain.

"Some things just aren't easy to talk about," she said. "I understand. I don't talk about my mom much, either. Or about how my dad left us." His eyes shot to her face, his brow furrowing. "And yet...you know more about my mom and my situation than anyone. I guess, for both of us, this is a trade-off. Everybody has a past. Some are just a little more unpleasant than others."

He nodded, grimly. "Yeah. Maybe." He offered up a ragged smile before deftly changing the subject. "So, about this coat. Consider it an early Christmas gift. Or a payback. Kind of like barter. We're helping each other get what we want. Maybe this year, it's the only way to suffer through Christmas."

Chapter Six

Something snapped in Jared after he'd unwittingly given Nicki a glimpse of his fears. He started feeling better about himself, about the whole prospect of bringing his child home again. It was kind of prophetic. Sandra had taken Maddy away at Christmas, and now she was sending her back at the same time.

He guessed, deep down in his gut, that Madison didn't really want to come back. And he couldn't blame her. They didn't know each other. The divorce two years ago had upended Madison's stable, secure world. This past year Sandra had moved every few months, and if anything went wrong in her life, she blamed Jared for it. He'd probably been portrayed as some vicious ogre, a being so far removed from the loving father that is every child's dream daddy that Madison would probably arrive in Winter Park anxious and withdrawn.

He just wanted her to be happy…and he knew, as much as he hated to admit it, that Nicki had all the qualities he needed to bridge the gap and to make that happen.

St. Nick, as he most often referred to her, had an incredible smile, one that made her eyes go soft and luminous. As if there was a little candle light glowing from the bottom of her soul. She was a woman who was spiritually kind. The woman who keeps on giving—like a clock that keeps on ticking.

It was probably intrinsic in her genetic makeup. Either that, or a flaw. Men, without realizing it, used women like that. He couldn't help wondering what kind of men had passed through her life. She'd dismissed her reference to her father, saying simply that he'd left them. It wasn't hard to figure he'd left them high and dry. She'd never mentioned a boyfriend, a significant other, or an ex.

It really didn't matter, save for the fact he intended to monopolize her time for the next few months—and he didn't want anyone else muddying up the picture. He was paying for her time, and he inexplicably found himself wanting all of it. Maybe that was why he'd demanded she move in as quickly as possible.

Sure, he'd told her it was prudent to install her in his home—to save her the inconvenience of running back and forth, to get her life in order—and close up the condo and all that. But it rankled him, thinking of her in that antiseptic condo, knowing she wanted to get rid of it, knowing she had some sad memories she wanted to put behind her.

He could see it in her, how she wanted to get on with her life. She tried so hard, desperately hard. Look at how she was throwing herself back into the holidays. He suspected it was because she was trying to ease the pain of losing her mom. He knew, from what little she'd said, that her mom was all the family she had left.

Now she was alone in the world. Kind of like him.

The kiss they'd shared on the dance floor the night of the gala had rocked him. He thought about it at the strangest times. When he was going over orders for small appliances, when he was meeting with his paunchy CEO, or eating Chinese takeout from a cardboard carton. The impact of that single kiss amazed him.

He hadn't believed he was capable of feeling that kind of physical reaction. For a moment he'd almost forgotten who he was and what he was doing. The world had closed up and swallowed him whole, leaving only Nicki and those precious little sounds she made when he'd parted her lips.

A few days ago, when he'd looked at her through the department store mirror, he considered how easy it would be to turn her around and persuade one more small intimacy from her tempting mouth. Another kiss. A little thank-you for the coat, he'd irrationally rationalized. A payment he genuinely didn't want to receive.

Yet his body betrayed him, offering up dual reactions. He didn't want emotional involvement, didn't want to recognize the silky invitation of her walnut-dark hair or the low gurgle of seduction he knew she could offer. He didn't want to press himself against her soft curves. Yet he'd memorized the sway of her perfect breasts as she'd bent to pick out those prints. Later, he'd used that blasted coat as an opportunity to splay his hands around her tiny waist, allowing his fingertips to ease onto the flare of her hips.

In the kaleidoscope of his imagination, he saw his hips bumping up against hers. He saw his limbs tangling with hers—knees bumping against thighs, her forearms pressing against his back, the arch of his foot tracing the sexy curvature of her calf. Sheets twining and twisting around them both. Silk sheets, satin sheets. Feather beds or water beds.

The woman was driving him crazy, tormenting him with lurid, taunting visions.

He wanted her. Or else he simply needed the intimacy of a sexual encounter. His body physically ached for a woman—and St. Nick aroused something in him he hadn't felt for a long, long time.

He intended to put a lid on it. Tamp it back down and remind himself he wasn't going there again, not with a woman who made him feel something.

Once she'd done her job, and Madison was the happy, healthy, well-adjusted little girl he wanted, she was out of here. Jared Gillette got custody, and Nicki Holliday got a handsome severance check. In the end, it would all work out. And certainly for the best.

Jared pulled in to the drive, a smidgen of guilt shredding his mind. It was the middle of the week, and he'd knocked off early. Something he never did, not during the Christmas season.

Irene was in the kitchen, up to her elbows in dishwater. Something smelled heavenly. Wednesday night. Pot roast, and all the trimmings. Fresh-baked bread.

"How do you do it?" he asked, dropping his briefcase on the island and shouldering out of his coat to drop it over the bar stool. "How did you know I'd be here early?"

She half turned, and arched a brow at him, rearranging some of the pulp in her round, mottled face. "I didn't. But some of the people around here could sure stand to eat on time, and put a little meat on their bones."

He frowned, confused.

"That child's working too hard," she said crossly. "Lugging boxes in and out all day. Trampin' through the house. Packing, unpacking. Hauling that furniture around upstairs as if she worked for a moving company. More's the pity, me seein' people what's got to work that hard around here. People just tryin' to make a wage."

Jared stopped short, taken aback by his housekeeper's barrage. "St. Nick? I told her I'd get someone to do the heavy stuff."

"Apparently she ain't waitin'," Irene grumbled. "This here dinner's for her. You want some, you get yourself a plate."

"Okay—" he started for the cupboard "—I can do that."

"You want to eat nice," she interrupted, wringing out a dishrag, "you carry the whole shebang into the dining room. Might as well get some use out of them nice Irish linen napkins your mama was partial to."

"Well, we've got some napkins right..." He pulled out the box of paper napkins.

She stared at him, pursing her lips, as if she dared him to defy her.

"We can use real napkins," he amended, sliding the box back onto the shelf, "as long as you don't mind the extra ironing."

"You ever hear me complain?" she flung back at him, wiping her hands on the embroidered tea towel.

He shrugged, and stacked the plates, putting the flatware and two water glasses on top before he started for the dining room.

"And light them candles on the table while you're at it," she said. "Makes a person relax a little and feel good at the end of a long day."

He turned around, intending to argue that the one thing he didn't need at the end of the day was some flickering little flame dancing around a cavernous room, barely shedding any light on his food.

Then it hit him. She didn't give a hoot what he wanted. The woman was thinking only of St. Nick, and her comfort.

Oh, God help him, Irene actually liked St. Nick. He was in trouble now.

"Dinner will be on that table in a half hour," she said, pausing at the stove to lift the lid off a pot and peer inside. "Now get out of my kitchen. And, in the meantime, go see what you can do to help that child."

Jared, somewhat grateful to be banished from the kitchen, quickly went into the dining room. He tossed the plates on the table and intentionally put the tableware awry. By the time he pulled the linen napkins out of the buffet, and plopped them beside the plates, he was thoroughly annoyed.

He didn't eat with the help. He ate by himself. He didn't eat off the dining room table anymore, he ate off the coffee table, in front of the TV. He didn't use real napkins or candles. He used disposable paper products, and 100-watt bulbs. He didn't want intimate conversation, he wanted dead silence.

Crud. Having another woman under his roof was already making a mess of his life. Okay, so he'd indulge them. Just this once. One time, and one time only.

He grudgingly placed the two water glasses near the plates, and determined that he'd use tonight's dinner to give St. Nick a few last-minute instructions on Madison's arrival. He'd outline the game plan for her, just so there were no surprises. He'd tell her what he expected in no uncertain terms. He'd delineate the importance of taking care of a child, his child. He'd explain, firmly, that he didn't eat with the help.

Then he stalked upstairs to set his plan into motion.

He was six steps from the door to the nursery when he heard Nicki groan.

"Ohh-hh...I can't...um-mm, yes...higher..."

What? The most ridiculous image torpedoed through his head...and exploded right below his belt buckle.

He quickened his pace, then halted at the open nursery door. "What, exactly, is it you think you're doing?" he demanded.

Nicki, balancing on tiptoe on the seat of a straight-backed chair, startled then swayed. She looked over her shoulder at him. "I—I can't get this up there..." she explained breathlessly before her knees buckled and her hips shifted. Her shoulders thunked against the wall, and the print she clutched slithered down her middle. "You scared me!" she accused, her chest heaving.

When her eyes shuttered closed, and she was safely braced against the wall, he strode over to her. Without giving it a second thought, his palms spanned her waist. Her eyes flew open.

"What're you...?"

"I'm helping you down before you hurt yourself." He effortlessly swung her down. Yet the gesture grated on him, and he endured another reminder of how lithe, how supple, the woman was. To top it off, he got a damn hitch in his groin. A sexual hitch.

"I didn't plan on that, not until you snuck up on me and—" She chopped off the explanation and hefted the print in his direction. "I wanted to get these hung before you got home, but I couldn't reach, and..."

"Here." He took it from her, offering up his best imitation of an irate employer, and nudged the chair out of the way. He jammed the print against the wall, above the other three. "You want it where?"

"A little to the right," she said shakily.

He moved it.

"No, a little higher."

He moved it again.

"A little more."

He glared down at her, then lifted the frame another quarter inch.

"Perfect," she praised, her voice growing stronger, her fear of falling long past.

Suddenly the most profound irony struck him and his lips twisted. Then he snorted. Marking the spot with his thumb, he waited while she exchanged the print for a hammer and nail. He smacked the nail once, sinking it deep in the plasterboard. Satisfied, he took the framed print she offered, and hung it above the others.

They both stepped back to study the four carefully arranged prints.

Finally his head swiveled in her direction. "Do you consider it strange, Nicki, to realize that—somehow—I've ended up working for you?"

Nicki's eyes widened, to expose clear blue irises.

Oh, roll those baby blues, he thought absurdly.

Then her jaw slid off center, diverting his attention to her quivering lips, the pale tinge of cherry gloss staining them.

"I didn't know where to find a ladder," she explained,

"and I didn't want to bother your housekeeper again. I've made a nuisance of myself so many times already."

"Yes, well, you aren't going to be much help to any of us if you fall off a chair and break your leg or something."

"I wasn't planning on it. In fact, I was doing just fine, until you came in to help."

He ignored her pique. "I can see you've..." His eyes trailed the room. Boxes, all marked, were stacked against the far wall. The closet hung open, the racks emptied of the tiny baby gowns, the christening dress, the bonnets and sun suits and playsuits. The bright-colored toddler toys were gone, and in their place were board games and fashion dolls and a pale pink CD player. Jared's heart wrenched. "You've done a lot of work," he said finally.

The crib and bassinet and changing table had mysteriously disappeared, and in their place stood a twin-size bed. It was already made up, the softly swirled teal comforter, folded back at one corner to expose matching sheets embellished with tiny pink hearts. Regular pillows, heart-shaped, and bolsters in the same matching fabric were artfully arranged on the mattress.

"They delivered the bed today," Nicki explained needlessly.

"I see that," he mused. The oak sleigh bed, with its curved footboard and delicately carved headboard, resembled a safe haven. It was a good choice. Solid. Secure. Special.

"Is it okay?"

"It's fine."

"The other pieces will be delivered later in the week."

"Fine." He glanced at the bookshelves, and instinctively knew that the ABC books were gone. He noted that in their place, several large-print, beginner reader books scattered the top.

God, he'd missed so much.

"I didn't get rid of anything," Nicki said softly. "If you want it, I have it all labeled, and I can find it in an instant.

Really. There were so many beautiful things, but I wasn't sure which ones were the most special to you, so..."

His attention flickered back to her face. She was concerned—and for the first time he noted the dark circles under her eyes. She had been working overtime. Both at her home and his.

He shook his head. "Nothing's special to me," he said emphatically. "Nothing. Besides, I told you to box it all up. I'm just amazed at what an incredible job you've done, and in such a short time."

A hesitant smile wobbled on her mouth, and for one insane instant he wondered what he could do to bring her dimples into full focus.

"How are things going at the condo?" he asked.

"I'm getting rid of some of the furniture, tying up loose ends. I brought a bunch of boxes over today. It's funny the things that stop you when you go through stuff. I pick up a magazine and think about how my mom told me to read this article, or I pick up the silver letter opener from the Chicago World's Fair and think of how my mom opened every single envelope that came into the house with it." Nicki sighed, her expression sad. "It's slow going," she admitted. "I should have had you come over and clean out my place. I mean, fair's fair. It's probably easier when there aren't any memories attached."

It was in him to shrug off the sentimentality, but he couldn't bring himself to do it. "Yeah, it's funny how a—" he struck "stranger" from his explanation "—how someone else can go through your stuff so casually. They take it at face value, I suppose."

"I didn't think it would be this hard, you know."

She lifted her face to his for confirmation, and Jared, mesmerized by her honest sincerity, fell victim to her innocence, and said the first thing that popped into his head.

"No, neither did I, St. Nick. Neither did I."

They tarried over the meal and, somewhere in the middle of it, Jared realized he hadn't been this relaxed in years.

He watched Nicki's animated face, bathed in candlelight, and didn't give the store or his responsibilities a second thought. Stress slid off his shoulders, and dripped off his fingertips—right onto the Irish linen napkins.

He leaned both elbows on the table, and pushed his plate aside. "So tell me about what you did before you were a Santa Claus," he said. "Some art department or something I read in your file?"

"I was an illustrator. I did sketches for a greeting card company."

"Impressive. No wonder you're so creative."

She smiled modestly, her dimples doing their job. "Everyone has some kind of talent. Mine just happened to be drawing. I spent a lot of hours doodling when my mom worked."

The housekeeper came into the dining room clucking, a silver tray of desserts held high above her shoulder. "What?" she said, fixing Nicki with a stare. "You too tired to eat? You barely touched that pot roast."

"Not true," Nicki protested, dropping her hand across her stomach. "I'm stuffed. I haven't had a meal like that since..."

The housekeeper waited expectantly.

Nicki tried to finish the sentence, then stumbled.

Jared intervened. "Since mom's home cooking?" he asked.

Appearing relieved, Nicki shot him a grateful smile across the table. "Yes. Since that."

"Well, now, that's fine," Irene unabashedly approved. "Pleased to know I'm in good company. Imagine your mama was a fine woman, to raise a sweet child like you." She brought the tray down, ignoring Nicki's flush of embarrassment. "Dessert's a bit of a surprise. Figured I ought to get started on our Madison's arrival." She placed the tray of outrageously decorated sugar cookies in the center of the table. Bells, stars, Christmas trees, candy canes, Santa

Clauses and reindeer. They swirled with icing and colored sugars, cinnamon candies, and silver balls.

Nicki visibly swooned.

Even Jared smiled.

"Oh, my…"

"I haven't had these in years."

The housekeeper made a show of boxing his ears—or at least acting as if she intended to. "Because you haven't paid a lick of attention to what's been on your plate, that's why. No sense wasting my time on someone who's just going to fork down my good food and then mumble through it."

Jared sheepishly reached for a cookie.

"Kind of nice to have some real conversation in the house tonight," Irene went on. "I expect, once that child gets here, this will be an everyday occurrence, having everyone sit down to dinner and all."

The sugared bell Jared was about to bite into stopped midair. *For whom the bell tolls,* he thought sagaciously. He straightened, prepared to offer Nicki a significant look, and to put a stop to this fraternizing. "Yes, well…about that…"

"Children need to have that," the housekeeper intoned over his shoulder. "No sense eatin' on the fly. Children need to be around people they trust, people they spend time with, especially at dinner. Mealtime's the most important part of the day."

Jared stared at that damned cookie and closed his mouth. He knew, just knew, that if he said anything now, he'd get a crumb stuck in his throat and choke.

Huh. He had moments when he wanted to throttle Irene. This was one of them. Her and all her sugar-coated philosophy about how to raise children and be a family.

His gaze met Nicki's. Her eyes still on him, she reached over and carefully selected a Santa Claus cookie. When she put it to her lips, he suffered another hitch in his groin. Then, still smiling, she daintily nibbled off the head.

The significance was not lost on him. *So long Santa Claus, hello life.*

Jared immediately felt his chest loosen up and an indescribable feeling of mirth filled him. He wanted to roar, he felt so good. He wanted to eat at this damn table every night and have this confounded woman amuse him, and smile at him, and console him. He wanted to see the way she dabbed at her mouth with her napkin, or gazed at him over the rim of a water glass. He wanted to see if she cut her veal into little tiny pieces, or used catsup on her eggs. It wasn't right, but that's the way it was.

"Nicki," he said. "It appears my housekeeper has a point. I'll have to insist on your presence every night at dinner. To oversee Madison, of course."

"Humph! 'Bout time," the housekeeper uttered before she waddled back into the kitchen.

Chapter Seven

The entire household revolved around Madison's imminent arrival. Jared worked longer hours at the store, so that he could personally pick her up at the airport. Dividing her time between her condo and his home, Nicki diligently put both their lives in order.

There had been moments when Nicki feared she wasn't doing things to Jared's satisfaction, yet when she asked him about it, he brushed it off, saying everything was "fine." She began to detest that word. Apparently the strong, silent type threw that word around a lot, without any real enthusiasm or conviction.

Still, since he wasn't being critical, she went ahead and kept on doing what she was doing, telling herself that nothing could be better than seeing Christmas through the eyes of a child. This would be her home for Christmas, and she intended to enjoy it, to celebrate and share in the warmth of people who loved each other.

She'd persuaded Jared to let her set up a real tree in the family room, next to the fireplace. At first he'd argued the spindly, artificial one she'd unearthed in the basement was good enough for a couple of weeks. But she'd convinced him the scent of pine would be good for their souls, the real pine needles longing for a child's handcrafted ornaments. He'd caved in, saying, "Fine, do it if you have to."

For the mantel, Nicki purchased inexpensive stockings to decorate with glitter and braid. When she'd shown them to Jared, he'd again said, "Fine," then reminded her if she really thought they needed stockings, she could have gotten something in Gillette's and saved herself the trouble. Not as much fun, she admonished, not when children love to glue and paste and make something from nothing.

It was then he ultimately uttered the final, "Fine, do whatever you want."

And she had.

After she finished Madison's room, she totally immersed herself in Christmas preparations. There were childish holiday tunes on the CD player, and classic movies stacked next to the DVD player. Peppermint candies were in the candy dishes and eggnog waited in the refrigerator. An animated Santa Claus was installed in the foyer, to belt out a merry "Ho, ho, ho" to every passing visitor. Three red sleds found a home in the garage—in case Winter Park received a dusting of snow.

Christmas, Nicki decided happily, was the best possible time for a reunion—and she intended to make this reunion between father and daughter poignant. Doing things for them, anticipating their joy and happiness, took the edge off of her own sorrow and loneliness.

Sometimes as she worked she thought about her own father, and wondered if he ever missed her, or ever regretted walking out. Her mother once said he'd gone to Alaska to work on the pipeline and had remarried, so she knew she'd never see him again. He'd never sent her so much as a birthday card. Of course, he'd never sent her mother so much as five dollars for groceries, either.

Funny, there was a world of difference between her fa-

ther and Jared. It helped to know that even though some
men like Jared didn't show it, they did care.

Jared had been silent, almost gruff, about the emotional
backlash of her move and closing up the condo. He had
effectively skirted all mention of her mother. He never
asked why her father had left. She'd stoically told herself
that it was because he didn't know what to say, because
while he was getting his daughter back, Nicki had to go it
alone. She yearned to talk to him, but there were times he
seemed so forbidding.

There was too much on his mind. The store, the joint
custody, the fact his ex-wife was getting married again. Any
of those issues would be enough to make a person irritable.

Yet, even as the tension between them escalated as Madison's visit became imminent, Jared tempered it with inexplicable bouts of kindness.

The man was an enigma, no doubt about that. If he saw
her struggling with boxes, he took them from her. If he
caught her singing along with the CD player, he smiled
indulgently, as if he *supposed* he could endure it. Yet, unless something was wrong, unless he had something specific
to share with her, he never sought her out.

Sometimes she paused to look at him, head bent, while
he worked, his briefcase open beside him, the lamp tossing
sparks over his blue-black hair, and she thought he was the
most handsome man she'd ever seen. Looking at him, when
he wasn't looking back, put the strangest little butterfly sen-
sations through her middle.

The way he spoke made her listen more intently. It was
so fascinating to watch the play of his mouth, the way his
perfect white smile would fade in and out. She'd lie awake
at night and try to memorize the honeyed timbre of his
voice, the cadence of his words. She repeated their conver-
sations in her head, often drifting off to sleep with the
sounds of his voice nuzzling her ear. And then she'd be
reminded of the time he'd kissed her....

The first morning she awoke in his home, she'd lain

awake and stared at the ceiling, thinking to herself that this was "his" bed she was sleeping in, "his" sheets she was sleeping on, "his" feather pillow she laid her head on. The realization had given her goose bumps, and she'd foolishly stroked the percale sheets and savored the scent, the texture, of them.

Everything she did brought her closer to Jared—and, for better or worse, he was always in the back of her mind.

The car pulled into the driveway at 2:22 p.m. Both the housekeeper and Nicki jockeyed for a better vantage point at the kitchen window. Jared got out first, his face weary. He went to the trunk and pulled out Madison's suitcase.

Madison, her long blond hair flying, skipped around the front of the car. She wore sandals, with socks, a pair of raggedy jeans and a baggy sweatshirt. She paused to kick at a stone in the driveway, then said something to Jared. He leaned down, resting his hand on her shoulder.

Nicki grinned. Madison appeared alert, animated, and very much the typical child.

The housekeeper pushed away from the windowsill and muttered, "From pillar to post, that's what I say. Now, we'll find out how much that high-and-mighty Miss Sandra cared about that young 'un."

Before Nicki could reply, the back door slammed against the wall.

"Madison," came Jared's mild reproof, "not so hard, please."

They came in together, Madison at Jared's side. She unabashedly looked the kitchen over, her eyes fastening on the cookie jar.

"Madison, you probably don't remember the housekeeper," Jared prompted. "But she remembers you. This is Irene. She made your baby food, and took you for rides in the stroller."

Madison bestowed a halfhearted look to the housekeeper. "Oh. Hi."

The housekeeper's smile widened and, over her broad girth, she bent to chuck Madison under the chin. "We're mighty glad to have you back, Madison."

Madison pulled back, and wrinkled her nose distastefully.

"And you haven't met Nicki," Jared went on. "She's a friend of mine, and she's staying here. She's going to spend a lot of time with you, to help you get settled, and all."

"Hello, Madison," Nicki greeted, extending her hand. Madison shook it, and Nicki noticed four cheap gumball rings had turned her fingers green. She vaguely wondered if gangrene could set in. "I've been looking forward to meeting you," she said. "I know we're going to have a lot of fun together."

"Okay. Sure," Madison said, dismissing Nicki as her eyes flitted to the refrigerator. "You got anything to drink around this place?"

If Nicki was startled by the abrupt, poorly phrased question, she refused to show it. She stepped up, knowing it was her job to see to Madison's needs. "It's been a long trip, huh? What would you like? We've got lemonade, juice, chocolate milk, and even some eggnog."

"What's eggnog?"

Pleased to be able to introduce the child to her first Christmas treat, Nicki couldn't beat back a smile. "It's a special Christmas drink. From milk and egg and nutmeg. I've been told it's Santa's favorite drink," she confided. "He always has a cup before he takes off in his sleigh on Christmas Eve."

"No kiddin'?" Madison said, intrigued, her brow furrowing. "Well, I'll take some of that."

The housekeeper handed Nicki a glass, and Nicki did the honors, pouring it half full. She started to bring it to the table, where Jared had her seated.

"I want a straw," Madison demanded.

Nicki stopped. "Oh. Okay..." She caught the housekeeper's eye, half afraid there wouldn't be a straw to be found in a three-mile radius.

"Right here," the housekeeper said, pulling a straw out of a nearby cupboard and dropping it into the glass.

Nicki placed it before Madison like a peace offering.

"Looks like a milkshake," she said happily, experimentally stirring the eggnog with the straw.

Three doting adults stood over the child as she took her first sip. She took a long noisy pull at the straw, then her head jerked back and she gagged. "This stuff sucks!" she said, spitting, and wiping her mouth with her sleeve. "What're you tryin' to do, poison me?"

All three adults scrambled to make things right.

"Here, don't spit it out," Jared said, whisking the glass away.

Nicki quickly offered Madison a napkin, then blotted at her sleeve with another. While she rubbed away the offending eggnog, she took note of the child's sweatshirt. Ketchup, mustard and chocolate were just a few of the identifiable stains. Grime was ground into the ribbing at the neck and sleeves, and the fleece was comfortably rumpled, as if Madison had slept in it. This close, her hair looked more tangled than curled, and there was actually dirt under her fingernails.

No wonder Jared looked distressed. His only child definitely looked the worse for wear, and just a notch short of neglected.

The housekeeper wiped at the table with a damp dishrag. "Let's get you something else," she suggested.

"No, I've had enough of that junk," Madison said, sliding down from the chair.

"Nicki can show you your room," Jared said in dismissal, "and I'll be up in a few minutes with your suitcase."

"Come on, Madison," Nicki invited, heading to the door.

Madison's eyes narrowed, her look—from Jared to Nicki calculating. "Are you trying to get rid of me?" she asked.

Surprise rippled through Nicki. "No. Not at all. We thought you'd like to see your new bed. I found some brand-new puzzles and some books and—"

"Whatever," she replied.

They trooped up the stairs and, to Nicki's disappointment, Madison didn't even give the Santa Claus in the foyer a second look.

When they reached the landing, Madison paused. "I don't remember this house. My mom and I left a long time ago. I think it looks like a hotel, because there are so many rooms, and all the doors are closed."

Nicki smiled. "Yes, I guess it does resemble a hotel. Your room is the last one down there, on this side, across from your daddy's."

Madison peered down the long, dark corridor. "Is that woman downstairs going to bring us food whenever we want it? Like room service?"

Nicki couldn't help but laugh. "How do you know about room service?"

"My mom uses it all the time. She don't like to cook."

Ah, the lifestyles of the rich and famous, Nicki thought to herself. "No. Irene won't bring you food. We eat together, down in the dining room."

"Bummer," Madison complained, walking away.

Saying nothing more, Nicki laid her hand on Madison's shoulder, to steer her to the right door; Madison stiffened and pulled away. "I'll find it," she said crossly.

Nicki walked behind her, as niggling thoughts that this was not going well burrowed into her mind.

Madison suddenly bolted and ran down the hall. She threw open the door, then stopped on the threshold. "Wow," she exclaimed. "Is all this stuff mine?"

"You're the only little girl who lives here," Nicki said, coming up behind her.

Madison moved into the center of the room, spinning, and looking directly up at the ceiling. Then she hopped dizzily on one foot, making it all the way over to the child's play table, bumping into it and upsetting the puzzle Nicki had carefully arranged. The pieces scattered; Madison looked at Nicki and laughed. She walked over some pieces and kicked others out of her way.

Nicki determined to not say anything, not yet. Teach by example, she thought, bending to pick some of the pieces up and put them back.

"Hey! Look at this," Madison said, pausing long enough to study the two cherub prints Nicki had hung at Madison's eye level. Nicki had learned quite by accident they were Jared's favorites.

"Your daddy picked them out just for you."

Madison looked at her rather strangely, then turned away, to the shelves where construction paper, paste, and blunt-edged scissors were arranged in tubs on the bookshelves. "Hey, you want to see something funny? You got any crayons?"

Relieved, Nicki fumbled to find the crayons as quickly as possible. Either Madison was hyperactive or had a short attention span. Maybe she was overly tired and overly stimulated. Drawing would help calm her.

"Here. How about these? You know…" she said, turning back to finish picking up the puzzle pieces before she grabbed some paper, "I love to draw. That's something we can do together." She picked up a few sheets of paper, then added a few colored pieces to the mix. Madison had her back to her, apparently still interested in the framed prints next to the table. "Madison?" she queried, folding her legs beneath her to slip into the child-size chair. "Don't you want to join me?"

Madison swung back, pivoting on her heel. "Look!" she demanded. "Look what I did!"

"What, sweetie?" Nicki followed Madison's impatient gesture, and her face drained of color. The expensive prints. The darling little cherubs, so carefully chosen, now looked like sideshow oddities, with handlebar moustaches and long, flowing goatees. Black crayon slashes ruined the prints, and Madison was definitely proud of her handiwork. Nicki's stomach turned over.

Madison giggled loudly. "Gotcha!" she said.

"Madison…I—w-we picked out those prints just for you. I don't think we can get crayon marks off…and your daddy will—"

"So?"

The horror of the situation struck her. "Why would you want to do something like that?"

"It was just a joke. Don't you get it? A joke. They look funny now. I like them better this way."

Frustration made Nicki's nerve endings tingle and her shoulders constrict. This was not what she bargained for. What Jared's daughter needed was either firm guidance or a good spanking. Of course, the spanking part wasn't endorsed anymore and disciplining someone else's child would be tricky.

At the rate they were going, Madison would spend a lot of hours in the time-out corner.

Gritting her teeth, Nicki pulled herself off the chair, and headed for the adjacent bathroom to get a washcloth. Dampening one corner, she debated whether she could wipe some of the crayon off. Maybe an eraser would work better.

What was she doing? she suddenly asked herself. She hadn't seen a child this rude and unruly in the entire two weeks she'd worked as a Santa Claus. It would be easier to tell Jared to have at it, and just quit.

Madison yelled from the other room. "Hey, lady! Hey, what's-your-name! Come here! Look what I'm doing!"

Violently jerking both the faucets to the off position, Nicki rushed into the bedroom.

Madison, at the end of the sleigh bed, her arms akimbo, walked across the footboard as if it were a balance beam.

Nicki gasped. "Madison. Don't!"

"Why not?"

"Because it's a brand-new bed. Because you'll scratch it."

She wheeled on the narrow piece of wood, teetering as she stared at Nicki, defying her. "So."

"Because you'll fall," Nicki went on, moving toward the child, her hands extended. "You might get hurt."

"No, I won't. Watch." That said, the child spring-boarded off the end and took a flying leap right into Nicki's arms.

Nicki clutched at her writhing body, staggering, and half afraid they'd both tumble to the floor. Behind her, she distinctly heard Jared clear his throat. Nicki, horrified, struggled to stand. She raised her eyes and turned to the door.

Jared's gaze, dark and brooding, met hers. His fury, barely contained, lit up the room.

Madison locked her legs around Nicki's middle, and attached herself like glue. "Hi, Daddy," she sang.

"Madison," he said firmly, "I don't ever want to see you on the furniture again."

"Yes, Daddy," she said meekly, her mouth rounding into a pout.

"Nicki, as for you, I've been called back to work, but I want to see you immediately in my office after I return. I assume you'll have everything under control by then."

Although Madison put her in a chokehold, Nicki managed to nod dumbly. It occurred to her she was probably losing consciousness. Why else would she agree to such a preposterous ultimatum? Why else would she stay?

After Jared left, Madison leaned back, surveying the damage she'd done. "So," she said, "are you gonna stick around or what?"

Chapter Eight

The afternoon was a disaster. Nicki had tried to interest Madison in unpacking her suitcase, but soon discovered the child had arrived with a motley collection of summer clothes, most worn out, or outgrown, and all despicably dirty. The ultimate revenge, Nicki thought soberly; send your child packing back to your ex, with an attitude and a suitcase of dirty clothes.

How in the world was she going to turn this around?

Gone were the visions of sugarplums dancing in her head. She was trapped, veritably trapped—with a five-year-old terror and a father whose surly attitude was not destined to improve.

The condo, her only refuge, was closed—the furniture given away or sold. She didn't have another job prospect on the horizon and she didn't have a car; she'd told the mechanic to sell it for scrap—and what she received for it was not even enough for a bus ticket out of here.

She dreaded, absolutely dreaded, facing Jared tonight. He was going to rake her over the coals, she just knew it.

Dinner had been a fiasco, but the housekeeper had finally

knuckled under to Madison's pleading, and taken away chicken, peas, and mashed potatoes—and replaced the plate with a peanut butter and jelly sandwich.

In two hours Nicki had managed to bathe Madison, wash her hair, and cut her bangs. Along the way, she discovered that the child didn't know any Christmas carols, not even "Jingle Bells," but she knew the whole raucous version of "Grandma Got Run Over By A Reindeer." She learned that Howie drank too much beer, and her mother liked partying better at the Spiral rather than the Soggy Bottom.

"How about a story before bed?" Nicki invited, pulling a book off the shelves.

"Nah. I'd rather just watch TV before I fall asleep. Most of the time I stay up and watch the late show. I like to sleep on the couch, too."

Nicki smiled, pleasantly, and refused to give in. "Not an option, Maddy. I can either read to you, or tuck you in."

Madison stared at her, obviously debating whether this was an argument she was going to win. "Oh, all right, I guess." Madison climbed up into the big bed and pulled the covers over her. She patted the spot beside her. "You're going to sit here, aren't you? That's the way they do it in the movies."

Nicki smiled. In spite of everything Madison had put her through, there was still an innocence about her. "Sure, I can do that. I'm glad you know how this storytime thing works."

"Mmm, my mom reads me the back off the cereal boxes, but that's in the morning. We don't do this night stuff. I usually have a baby-sitter at night—and you know baby-sitters, they always have their boyfriends over and they're busy with them."

"Interesting," Nicki commented, settling onto the mattress and wedging her shoulders against the headboard. "Mmm, you smell pretty after a bath," she said, looking down at Madison. She couldn't resist patting one of Madison's curls back into place. "And your hair is so pretty, too. You know, I think this story is about a little girl who has long blond hair, just like you.'' She showed Madison the book jacket.

In moments they were chuckling together over one little girl's search for the perfect star for the top of her Christmas tree. Though Madison's eyes were heavy, she intently studied each page, tracing the illustrations with her finger. When they turned the last page, she yawned. Nicki asked her if she liked the story, and she nodded.

''I hate to interrupt,'' Jared said from the doorway. He appeared tired, his expression bemused as he loosened his tie. ''But it's getting late, and I want to see you, Nicki.''

Nicki straightened. She pulled her shoulders off the headboard, then swung her feet down from the bed. ''We just finished the last page,'' she said hastily, ''and were looking at the pictures.

''Fine.''

Nicki rose. ''Good night, Madison, see you in the morning.''

Madison slid further under the covers, effectively avoiding any hug Nicki could give her. ''Don't forget you said we'd do the decorations for the tree tomorrow,'' she reminded her.

''I won't forget,'' Nicki replied softly, patting her arm. She put the book away, and moved toward the door, but Jared still stood there, blocking her escape. Hesitating, she sidestepped his bulk. ''Is there anything else?'' she asked, feeling strangely on the defensive.

''I'll meet you in your room. Ten minutes.'' He turned away, to head for his room.

Nicki stared at his broad back, unable to comprehend he hadn't said a word to Madison. ''Jared,'' she called after him. ''I believe you wanted to say good-night to your daughter?''

Jared pivoted on one heel, a quizzical expression running through his dark eyes. He tugged on his tie, freeing it from his shirt collar.

"Madison's waiting," she reminded him. "For you."
With that, she turned and walked down the corridor, to
await her fate.

Madison pulled the covers over her head and turned her
back on her father. The message couldn't have been any
more succinct and a knife twisted in Jared's heart. But what
could he expect, really?

"Good night, Madison."

Madison didn't move a muscle. Her face was to the wall.
It took everything in him, but he tried again. "I heard
you and Nicki are going to decorate the tree tomorrow."

She remained silent.

"Anything I can do to help you out with this tree-
decorating stuff?"

She jerked the covers around her neck as though she was
battening down the hatches, then she twisted beneath them
as if she couldn't quite get comfortable. Several seconds
slipped away. "Why would you care?" she asked bellig-
erently. "You left me here. You went back to work. You
don't care what I do."

So that was it. "Maddy, I wanted to be here with you
today. Really."

"Yeah. Right."

"I worked late last night, just so I could be the one to
pick you up at the airport." She flipped onto her back and
stared straight ahead, at the wall, where two prints, scarred
by her childish scrawls hung. "This is Christmas," he explained, "and it's the busiest time of the year at the store."
Her eyes flickered, and he hoped, fleetingly, that he was
getting through to her. "I didn't mean to make you feel
bad."

One finger wiggled out from beneath the comforter to
stroke the satin binding on the pillowcase. "You could have
called," she accused.

Jared sank a hip onto the bed, figuring this was the closest he was going to get to a concession or an invitation.

"You're right. I could have. How about if we make a date every day for me to call you? Say, three o'clock."

"Kind of like when I live in California and you live here?"

"Just like."

"Okay. I guess." Her shoulder leaned back toward him, just slightly, just enough to indicate she was open to the suggestion.

He paused, wondering what to say next. "How are you going to decorate the tree?"

"Candy canes and gumdrops and licorice whips."

"No?" He exaggerated the question. "You're decorating the tree, not planning to eat it?"

A hint of a smile played around her lips. "Daddy."

"So how do you like Nicki?"

Madison considered, her head tilting. "She's okay. But she made me play Candyland all afternoon."

"Made you?"

"I kept beating her, and she doesn't like to lose."

"Oh."

He was about to say good-night, when she said, "Daddy? Do you like Nicki?"

"Of course. She's fun, she's funny, and did you know she has a hotline to Santa Claus?"

Madison rolled her eyes, ignoring the suggestion. "No. I mean, do you like her like Mommy likes Howie?" Jared opened his mouth, then promptly closed it, aware of where this was leading. "You know, all that mushy stuff," she prompted.

"M-mushy stuff?" he repeated. Thoughts of the kiss he'd shared with Nicki on the dance floor made him uncomfortable. Memories of the encounter he'd orchestrated had plagued him for a week. Every time he looked at Nicki, he thought of it. "She's just a friend," he said, "that's all. And she's going to be staying with us for a while. Until you're situated, and she finds another job."

"She's not going to stay?"

Hearing an edge of hysteria in Madison's voice made Jared revise his statement. "Of course, she's going to stay. For as long as we want her to. For as long as it works out for all of us."

Jared didn't know what had come over him. He should be thinking about Madison, but instead he was thinking of Nicki.

Maybe it was seeing her all curled up with Madison, their heads together, whispering softly, as they turned pages and looked at pictures. Or it could have been Madison's inferences about "mushy stuff" that had done the job on his male hormones.

Life sure had a way of challenging a man's self-control. That, and his best intentions.

He loved his child dearly, but it would always grate on him that he'd chosen the world's worst mother for her. While he was talking to Madison, it had come to him in a flash that she actually needed someone like Nicki, someone who had her priorities straight, someone who knew how to laugh, and who knew what was important.

Sandra had duped him. Sometimes he didn't know if it was she who had changed the minute he'd slipped the diamond-encrusted ring on her finger, or if he had been foolishly blind to her hunger for money, to her quest for fun-loving irresponsibility. She had been delightfully impetuous at twenty-two, and self-serving and rash at twenty-five. When she wanted a child at twenty-seven, Jared had thought it was because she was ready to grow up—he'd never realized it was because she wanted, as had her other friends, a child to trot out at her convenience and show off.

Sandra had had all the qualities that could have taken her far in life—but she'd chosen not to use them, she'd chosen an alternate lifestyle he couldn't tolerate.

The only thing he truly regretted about the past his past—was that Sandra was not the woman he wanted as a wife or as a mother to his children.

Seeing Nicki like that...made him remember all his hopes for a big family, for a committed family grounded in principles, bound by loyalty. Now, he realized, that those were just high expectations cloaked in fantasy. You never got what you really wanted out of life, it would be absurd to think otherwise.

Still, the last few days, he hadn't treated Nicki right—and he knew it. He'd treated her like hired help because he couldn't fend off the stirrings she created in him. He'd told himself—wrongly—if he didn't see her, or talk to her, she couldn't affect him. If he dismissed her, she wouldn't come to him willingly, not about anything.

Yet he'd been conscious of her everywhere in the house.

She'd unwittingly started laying her brown leather purse on the kitchen chair nearest the window, and he'd have to move it because that was his favorite breakfast chair. At night he'd find her shoes paired outside the back door because she didn't want to track across Irene's clean floor, and he'd wind up bringing them in so they wouldn't be cold when she next slipped them on. Yesterday he'd opened the coat closet and found a familiar blue wool coat hanging next to his leather jacket. He'd pulled on the jacket, and realized, too late, the scent of her perfume lingered on his own clothing.

He couldn't escape her. And some days he didn't know if he wanted to.

His child had come home to him a heathen—unskilled in social skills and manners—and he had walked off and gone back to work, expecting Nicki to fix it, without complaint. The least he owed her was an apology. Or maybe an explanation.

After he'd left Madison's room, he hadn't gone directly to talk to Nicki. He'd gone down to the kitchen for a peace offering—and even that, he knew, wasn't a good idea.

He paused at the top of the landing and peered down the long corridor. Nicki's door hung open and light streamed into the hallway. He imagined her there, waiting, and his heart gave a little jump. He counted the steps to the door, then, with the back of his knuckles, rapped on the doorframe.

Nicki came around the corner. She'd taken off her cardigan sweater, and kicked off her shoes. Her blouse had been pulled from the waistband of her dark-colored dress pants. "Come in. Sorry for the mess," she said, indicating the packing boxes stacked just inside the door.

He shrugged, ignoring them. "You haven't had enough time for yourself."

Nicki's lips parted, as if she were surprised he'd noticed.

He tilted the bottle of wine in her direction. "This was supposed to be a fairly good year. I thought we could share it." She glanced at the date. It was recent, but she'd never grasp the implication. "The year Madison was born," he said, extending two wine flutes. "Back then it seemed pretty significant. As a parent you figure your firstborn is going to make a real impact on the world. Well—" he half laughed "—she certainly made an impact today, didn't she?"

Nicki avoided his eyes, and shrugged, her smile tight. "She did." Then, she backed up, and out of his way.

Jared indicated the kitchenette, and they both slipped into the tiny turn-around, standing side by side at the counter, their motions automatic. As he peeled the foil off the neck of the wine bottle, she set the flutes to the back of the counter, out of his way.

He concentrated on getting the cork out of the bottle. "Hard day?" he asked.

Nicki fiddled with the flutes. "We managed," she said carefully.

"I have to tell you, Nicki. This was not what I expected, not at all." From the corner of his eye, he watched Nicki nibble her lower lip. "It was a pretty rough start."

"I guess you were wrong about me, and what a whiz I am with kids."

He cleared his throat and reached for a flute. "We may

need to talk about how long you're going to stay, because—''

"Listen, about what happened to the prints, and her jumping off the bed, and—''

"Stop," he commanded, pouring the wine. "This isn't about that.''

"Jared, before you say anything else, I'll admit I wasn't doing my job. At least, not the job you hired me for.''

"What?'' Eyes narrowed, he looked at her, then set the filled flute aside.

"I know you're angry with me, I could see that this afternoon. You don't have to cover it by bringing in a bottle of wine and dulling my senses when you yell at me.''

"I didn't have any intention of dulling your senses," he said, frowning. "And I didn't have any intention of yelling at you.''

"You didn't come in here to fire me?''

"Hell, no. I came in here to beg you to stay.''

"I…''

"Don't tell me you didn't think about quitting a dozen times today," he accused.

Her attempt to laugh was pathetic, but her shoulders shook as if the irony was too much. "Where would I go?'' she said. "Everything I have is here.''

A corner of his heart twisted.

"Besides, have you ever tried to find a real job at Christmas?'' She chuckled at her own absurd question. It was common knowledge Jared's father built the store from the ground up, and had groomed his only son to take over the reins from the day he was born. "No, I guess not.''

"Nicki, stay here, with us, and I'll make it worth your while. Get the thought out of your head. I have no intention of firing you. Not twice.''

Her smile was strained. "You're sure about that?''

"Positive.''

"Okay, then I'll admit I thought about leaving. I thought about packing a suitcase and walking out the door. But…''

Nicki hesitated, chewing her lower lip. "Madison needs me. I realized, after you left, and I looked like an idiot and got over my initial shock, that she was testing me. Jared, she wanted to know if I'd stick around, no matter how mad she was."

Jared's fingers tightened around the neck of the bottle. His knuckles went white, and a feeling of helplessness rolled through him. "There's been a lot of people in and out of her life," he said, "Including me."

"It happens in a divorce," she said finally. "Somebody stays, somebody goes."

"The thing was, I stayed—and she should have stayed with me."

When Nicki laid her hand across his forearm, Jared flinched. He tried to tell himself the gesture was instinctive, but could only stare at her slim fingers and every ovaled nail.

"Don't be too hard on yourself," she said softly. "At least you invited her back into your life. You did more than my dad ever did. You just have to get to know her again. To feel comfortable with her again."

"Don't get the idea I'm beating myself up over this," he denied. "I'm not."

She dragged her hand from his sleeve. "And I'm not staying out of pity," she replied. "Not for you. Or Madison. I'm staying for myself, too. I'm being selfish."

"Why? Because you want to see if a dad and his daughter can actually reconcile."

Nicki grimaced as if he'd physically hurt her. Only then did he realize how deeply she hurt. "No," she said firmly. "I want a Christmas this year. A family Christmas. And yours is going to be it, whether you like it or not."

She extended the second flute.

Jared gazed at it momentarily, then started to pour as she held the glass. "What if I don't want to share?" he asked.

"But you will. And you know why? Because you need me. You said it yourself. You need me to bridge the gap.

And I made some progress with Madison today,'' Nicki said slowly, her eyes trained on the wine.

"I see that. A bath. Bangs that aren't hanging in her eyes.'' He twisted the bottle, and lifted it from the flute's rim. "Clean clothes, and a smidgen of trust.''

Nicki turned with the glass in her hand, to put the small of her back against the counter. She stared solemnly up at him. "Maybe the trust issues are genetic. Maybe she gets that from her daddy.''

Jared felt his eyes go flat, his mouth hard. He set the bottle down and picked up the other flute. "As for Madison,'' he said, clearly leaving himself out of the equation, "you have to understand that child is not the same little girl who left here two years ago. I had no idea—none—that she'd gotten so out of hand.''

"How could you?''

"I should have figured. Sandra's parents indulged Madison shamelessly, but they offered her a sense of family, of security. That was something I couldn't give her, not with the store and all my responsibilities. After they died, Sandra sold their home and started moving around a lot. I should have stepped in sooner, and brought suit against her for custody. But I didn't want to do that, I didn't want to put Madison in the middle of something that had the potential to get ugly.''

"Jared?'' He inclined his head, but didn't look at her. "I'm sure you made the best decision you could at the time. There aren't any blueprints for this kind of thing.'' Nicki paused, and pensively twirled the flute between her fingers. The wine lapped the rim. "My dad left us when I was six years old. He never came back. He never wrote, he never called.''

Jared paused. "I wondered. You never really said.''

"I don't like to talk about it. My mom lost everything. We lived in this nice house in a small town, and all she could find was a waitressing job. She thought it would get us through, until he sent money or came back.'' She half laughed and shook her head. "It didn't happen, Jared. My father never even cared enough to come back." She raised the glass, nearly to her lips. "Give yourself some credit, Jared. At least you were man enough, father enough, to want your daughter back. I have to admire you for that."

He studied her expression, searching for a scrap of bitterness, anger. Nothing. But her mesmerizing dimples had fled, and her eyes were vacant of any emotion. Odd, he thought he was the only one who had the corner on betrayal.

"This can have a happy ending," she predicted. "Maddy's only testing you. To see if you still want her, no matter what." She let her words sink in. "Take it from someone who knows, Jared. This can be fixed, and you can be the one to fix it."

For a moment he didn't know what to say. Finally he simply lifted his flute. "To Madison," he whispered hoarsely, "may we find a way to mend her broken heart and tame her wild spirit."

"Together," Nicki said, raising her glass to his.

The *ping* of the crystal provoked something deep and profound in the area of his heart. Nicki's single confirmation—*Together*—echoed in his head.

He wanted to reach for her, so very, very badly. His hands trembled when he raised the flute to his lips—for he wanted instead to drink of Nicki's softness, to taste her wine, to immerse himself in her own unique bouquet. He wanted to lose some of his pain, and to absorb hers.

As he sipped the wine, the most absurd rationalization popped into his head: maybe he just wanted to thank her, for all she'd done, and all she'd shared.

Wet from the wine and parted, her lips looked so kissable. Her blouse was loose, the two top buttons undone, and her dark hair, slightly tousled, seemed to call like a siren for a man to thread his fingers through it. There were always beckoning curls at her temple, her nape.

Jared acted on sheer impulse.

He set the flute on the counter, and took hers from her

hand. "Thank you for today," he whispered, leaning over her and losing himself in her azure-blue irises.

His mouth sought her cheek, for a mere gesture of appreciation. But it came as a shock, how warm and pliable her skin was. He couldn't get enough, and a heady need filled him, driving him, to seek her lips, to graze his tongue against hers.

Passion whorled, spinning an invisible net that bound them against each other. Her arms slid against his ribs, her palms resting flat against his back. He leaned into her middle, experiencing ecstasy when her breasts, curvy and firm, brushed his chest.

The kiss deepened, experimentally. The more he pushed, the heavier her weight became. He ached to lift her, possess her. His hand lifted, to the warm underside of her breast, his fingers instinctively burrowing against her flesh.

When she uttered the most involuntary, most incredible little noise in the back of her throat, he groaned. He went hard all over, with want, with need, with a passion that was spiraling out of control.

His hand cupped her breast, and she arched, her mouth slipping from his as she dragged in a deep, rasping breath. His thumb stroked higher, questing for the firm tip. Beneath the fleshy pad of his thumb, he felt her nipple tighten and go hard.

Without a shred of rational thought his fingers sought the buttons on her blouse, and he freed them, pushing back the fabric, to expose a delicate lacy bra, and skin so pure, so firm and beautiful that he wanted to absorb it, to bring it into himself. He wanted to taste, and to touch, and to explore. His forefinger moved under one silken strap and she quivered, feeling like an odd combination of velvet, of warm, pliable gelatin.

She moved, ever so subtly, and his body reacted in an effort to synchronize his movements with hers. Pressing his hips, his thighs, against her, his mind warned that he should pin her to the counter, to prevent her response—not to encourage it.

Yet his body moved with a will of its own, instinctively seeking satisfaction, and intent on slaking a deep-seated need. Dipping beneath the lacy cup of her bra, he gently caressed her breast, stroking dangerously close to the peak.

She moaned, her head falling back and putting the slim column of her neck, the curve of her jaw, at his mouth. He lifted his head to nibble her earlobe, pressing soft, persuasive kisses just below her ear. Then, with his tongue he traced a wet, slick path to her collarbone. She shuddered, moving involuntarily toward his searching fingers, his probing tongue.

"Jared," she muttered hoarsely, the word lost against his hair.

He was close enough to hear her heartbeat. It was strange, to hear his name rattle around in her lungs, her chest, mingling with the short spurts of her labored breathing. She smelled like vanilla and sweet wildflowers. No aphrodisiac could have been more intoxicating.

Lazily hooking a finger beneath the strap of her bra, he fully intended to take it down, to free her to his tongue, and the ravenous hunger that drove him. Just as he imagined taking her breast in his mouth, imagined laving at the rosebud-pink nipple, she shuddered.

"Jared...I haven't..." She made that crazy little sound again, and his eyes shuttered closed. "...Ever...."

...*Haven't ever*... The phrase tumbled seductively through his brain.

As if he'd been doused with a bucket of cold water, Jared yanked back, taking in clear, cleansing breaths, before he lost it all. Pulling her close, he stood over her, cradling her in his arms before his forehead sank against hers.

He couldn't let her go. Not yet.

His breathing wasn't right, and he knew it. "That shouldn't have happened," he said, fighting to put his voice on an even keel. "I'm sorry."

"It's just—I don't…do that. Not casually or—"

"Trust me, Nicki, I don't, either." He felt her tremble, as if she, too, were fighting to fling off the silken threads of ardor.

"I suppose it's easier to say no, if no one makes you feel…" She ducked her head, obviously saying more than she intended. "It's…okay. Forget it. Maybe we both needed a little comfort. This was not what we expected. Not for either of us."

He wondered at the double meaning, and pulled his shoulders back, away from her breasts. When he did so, he knew, through the sheer fabric, that her nipples remained taut and round with want. He swallowed, convulsively, refusing to think of what she must look like completely freed from her blouse, freed from the wispy binding of her brassiere. He banished the image from his mind: how his hand had touched her there, cupping her, exploring the peaks, the valley.

His lips twisted. "Comfort?" he asked. "Nicki, there's degrees of comfort. And we sure as hell went past that. From here on out, I'd recommend that we both indulge in a good wallop of self-control."

Chapter Nine

Nicki tried to clear her head. Yet all she could see was Jared's hard-core good looks. The slash of his brow, the cleft in his chin. Since this morning, when he'd last shaved, his day-old beard had become coarse and dark. He'd kissed her, and the stubble chafed her cheek. The flesh on her neck and chest tingled, offering up a painful reminder of far more intimate kisses.

He'd felt so good against her that she wanted to cling to him. She wanted some of his strength, just as she wanted to neutralize his arrogance with her own innocence. He was strong, and hard, and sculpted in all the places her hands wanted to discover. She wanted to pull his head down between her breasts, she wanted to writhe against him—even though she knew it wasn't safe, or sane, or sensible.

She should be shocked and embarrassed. She never told anyone about her absent father, she never divulged intimate details about her life. She never went around kissing, or touching, or going past the boundaries.

What was it about Jared Gillette that made her surrender?

He had become an uncanny force in her life, stripping her down to nagging thoughts and reckless behavior.

The moment was nothing but awkward.

"I know you're my boss. I know that," she said with more vehemence than she felt.

The reluctance with which he pulled away from her was obvious. "And that's why it shouldn't have happened," he said firmly. "I live by a strict code of ethics, especially for employers and employees."

It was a struggle to laugh, but she managed it, clutching the front of her blouse with one hand. "You don't have to tell me. I have firsthand knowledge of that."

The intensity in his features, the nerve throbbing along his jaw, the grim line of his brow, told her he wasn't going to back down. Or be swayed into making light of this uncomfortable situation.

"It won't happen again," he said, brushing her hands away to rebutton her blouse. "Not like that." When he finished, he sank back on his heel, imperceptibly putting more distance between them. "It's obvious we connect on…certain levels. But they have to remain centered on Madison. That's all there is."

"I understand that."

He shook his head so violently his perfectly sheared hair tumbled forward, splaying across his forehead. "No. I don't think you do."

"I know she's your first concern. I do."

Jared skimmed her with an anguished look. "My first marriage," he said, "was nothing short of a disaster. It was a relief when Sandra walked out—and I promised myself then to keep my life simple. No commitments, no involvements. Not even a fling. I don't get close to anybody, Nicki. Not even you."

The air around them went electric, white-hot, and throbbed with tension.

Nicki steeled herself, refusing to let him see how much his words hurt. "It must be a horrible way to live, Jared," she said softly. "Not ever giving anybody, not even your-self, a second chance."

A flicker of disbelief went through his ebony dark eyes. "It's the way *I* live," he announced. "And it will be better for both of us to keep it that way."

"Jared—"

"No," he said harshly. "With Madison in between us we have to be friends—and we *can* be that—but we never go beyond it. Never again."

Living in Jared's house was not easy. Especially after his ultimatum. There were simply too many reminders. Nicki saw him in everything she did. She couldn't walk by his leather chair without seeing the creases he'd put in it. The gold Cross pens he used to write with were always scattered across his desk, or next to his chair on the end table. *JG*—the monograms on his towels, inside his cashmere coat, his briefcase. The huge carafe of poppy seed salad dressing the housekeeper made especially for him. Even the Sunday newspaper inserts, with the Gillette's ads, were a reminder.

She began to see his traits in Madison. Worse, she began to look for them.

The way Madison frowned, the way she drummed her fingers when she was frustrated or pulled her ear when she was concentrating. Her penchant for orange juice; her dis-taste for broccoli.

There were so many things about him no one knew—and which she coveted. The way he paused at old black-and-white movies when he went through the cable channels. How he filled the bird feeder every other day, no matter how cold or dark or miserable it was outside.

Two days ago the housekeeper had sent Nicki on an er-rand to his library to find a blue folder. She'd discovered, quite by accident, a printout of his most recent charitable contributions. Toys for the foster care program, personal care items for the women's shelter, canned goods for the food pantry, clothing for community services. The list was endless.

The man was the devil-incarnate businessman by day and an angel of mercy by night. Either that, or his financial advisor was working overtime to get as many tax write-offs as possible.

Nicki experienced a consuming need to know who this man was, to know what he believed in and why. Sure, he'd told her that he didn't want to get involved, but his acts of charity belied his words. His tolerance and patience with Madison disproved his vow to remain uncommitted to anything or anyone.

Maybe a child was different, she idly told herself at night when a vision of his face tormented her and she remembered, too vividly, what it was like to kiss him. *To surrender in his arms, to melt against him. To crave another human being.*

Maybe, to Jared Gillette, a child was responsibility, obligation.

Of course, as her mother had always said, blood was thicker than water.

Nicki, obviously, was just a dash of rainwater on Jared's privileged life—a minor inconvenience to be brushed aside and quickly forgotten.

She tried to remind herself of that every time she stood in the background and watched as Madison ran to him and hugged his knees when he walked in the door. Clutching her latest art project to seek his approval, Madison would look over her shoulder and grin at Nicki when he complimented her cotton ball snowman or macaroni necklace. He might acknowledge her presence at those times, but Nicki had to remind herself it meant nothing. Because when Madison was nowhere near, he kept his word: she was just hired help. He remained silent, aloof, and unapproachable.

Even though Nicki's heart went out to him, logic told her he had made his choice.

The only thing they had between them, truly, was Madison.

* * *

Nicki offered Jared a surreptitious glance, painfully aware of how pleasant it was to share a calm, leisurely dinner with him every night. It was almost like being a family. They sat down to dinner and talked about the day's events, they praised Madison's accomplishments, planned for the future, and tarried over dessert. A dad, a fill-in mom, and a child.

Of course, it wasn't all rosy. Madison still had moments where she remained hardheaded and stubborn. A trait not unlike her father's, Nicki mused silently, comparing the firm set of his jaw and the intensity of his dark gaze to Maddy's jutting chin and bright blue eyes. Yet, overall, things were going better with her. True, there had been minor skirmishes, but Nicki was certain they were headed in the right direction. Maddy never mentioned her mom, and she'd adjusted fairly well to the routine Nicki had established for her.

The rapport between Madison and herself was growing daily.

The bond between Jared and Madison was tangible—although they had moments they seemed to circle each other, as if waiting for the other's reaction.

"You know," Nicki said, offering back the dinner roll Madison had asked her to butter, "the Winter Park Zoo is having a huge event for Christmas. It's called the Zoobilie Celebration."

"Zoobilie...?" Madison tried the word on her tongue.

"Mmm-hmm. The paper said every building is lighted and there are tons of Christmas displays. They have a special exhibit of reindeer, and there's supposed to be thousands of lights. Something like fifty thousand."

"They do it every year," Jared explained. "It's become one of their biggest fundraisers."

"I'd love to take Madison. Or, if you want to go..." Nicki let the invitation dangle, knowing full well she could be in deep trouble for putting him on the spot. Or for mentioning it in front of Maddy. Still, she wouldn't be here forever, and when she was gone, there needed to be some kind of compromise between father and daughter. "I think it would be good for us, and so much fun. They're having Christmas carolers and sleigh rides and Santa Claus."

Jared stared at his plate.

"Can we, Daddy?" The anticipation in Maddy's voice was palpable. "Can't we see the reindeer, Daddy?"

"Maddy, this is the busiest time of year for me."

Maddy's face fell.

Nicki intervened. "Or...if you'd rather take her..." she suggested softly, "without me..."

Jared's head swiveled, as if her suggestion had caught him off guard. He slowly leaned back into his chair, crumpling his linen napkin beside his plate as he thoughtfully regarded Nicki. She experienced the same uneasy feeling she'd had the day he'd fired her from the store. "Somehow you keep making me make choices," he said, his voice low. "Are you goading me or prodding me?"

"No, I'll take her," Nicki said quickly, avoiding the question. "I'd love to. But I thought it might be something you'd like to enjoy with her."

Maddy, who couldn't have cared less which adult escorted her, jumped into the fray. "Daddy, come on! Can I go? I want to see Santa's reindeer! Nicki taught me all their names. Comet and Cupid and Donder and Blitzen—"

"Enough, enough." Jared held up a hand, stopping her before pinning Nicki with a see-what-you've-started glance. Before she could object, he growled, "This is the busiest time of the year at the store, everyone knows that."

Nicki and Madison looked at their plates and fell silent.

"And because of that, I think," Jared went on, his tone subtly changing, "that we should take some time off. Let's go tonight. All of us. Nobody stays home. I declare this a Gillette family holiday."

Maddy's jaw dropped. "Can Irene go, too?" she asked.

"No way," Irene announced, coming in from the kitchen. "They got themselves one smelly monkey house, I can tell you. So don't get the idea you're gonna drag my poor, arthritic bones around for them pleasantries. Now, the three of you want to go off and have a good time, I'm all for it." She skimmed Jared with a pointed gaze. "Prob'ly be good for you, too."

Jared slid his chair back from the table and started to rise. He picked up his plate and glass. "We'll help clean up the dinner dishes, and then go."

The housekeeper took them from him. "Just get out of here, and quit crowdin' up my kitchen, will ya? Skedaddle. Go on with ya. Go on and have some fun, you kids."

Nicki and Jared exchanged glances.

"Yeah!" Maddy shouted, jumping from the table to run up the stairs to her room to get her coat.

The housekeeper bustled a load of dishes out of the room.

"Well...if we're going," Nicki said, "I suppose we should think about warmer clothes. I'll get Maddy's snow-suit and—"

"St. Nick?" Jared stopped her, laying a hand on her arm.

Nicki's heart beat a staccato rhythm, and she was insanely conscious of his aftershave, the cuff links at his wrist, the cleft of his chin. She'd become so used to him calling her St. Nick she'd never even given it a second thought. But he hadn't touched her, not even in passing, in a week. And it was impossible to not remember his last intimate touch. "Yes?"

"Indulge me. Wear the red wool. I've never seen you in it."

"Excuse me?" Her mouth went dry. Conscious they were sharing the first real conversation alone since the night he'd brought the bottle of wine to her room, her gaze strayed to his lips. He'd left her with a need, an insatiable, man-woman kind of need—yet she knew he'd never acknowledge it. He'd go about his life, pretending this thing they had between them wasn't there.

Inside she felt fuller. Having him touch her again made her feel as though she belonged, as if she was an integral part of a family who cared about her.

"The coat," he prompted. "It just seems so appropriate. What with the reindeer, and the sleigh rides, and all."

She paused. "You actually want to be reminded of the fiasco that brought us together?"

The hint of a smile played at the corners of his mouth. "Of course. You'll always be my lady in red," he said softly.

"Ho, ho, ho," Nicki whispered conspiratorially. But deep inside, her heart raced. He'd remembered, and he acknowledged it, and that in itself was something.

They went to see the monkeys first. It was, Madison declared, exactly as the housekeeper had said—smelly. But that didn't dampen their enthusiasm. They strolled down paths lit by hundreds of luminaries, the overhead tree branches strung with thousands of twinkling lights. Madison walked between them, clinging to their hands and skipping with uncontained excitement.

Nicki felt herself genuinely laughing for the first time in weeks. The diversion was just what she'd needed. Still, it was agony, as the glow of the lights only made Jared look that much more handsome, that much more appealing. For a few moments she bought into the fantasy, wishing desperately that they were a real family, that he was just your average guy off the street.

There was a decided disadvantage in being attracted to the most sought-after bachelor in Winter Park, the man who had been brought up to believe the Gillette millions were nothing less than tradition. He couldn't go anywhere without being recognized, and the same people who nodded at him wound up giving her a curious once-over.

"We need peanuts," he suggested, stopping at a vendor's cart. He bought the biggest bag, then passed them around.

Nicki crunched open the shell, then tasted. "These are incredible," she marveled. "I've never had hot, roasted peanuts."

He chuckled and offered her another handful from the bag.

"Do monkeys really like peanuts?" Madison asked, struggling to open the shell.

"Only monkeys like you," came Jared's quick reply.

"Daddy. Quit it. You tease all the time."

"Do not.

"Do, too."

"Do not."

"Daddy!"

He laughed. "You know what we need? A sleigh ride," he said, ushering them to the entrance. "That would make tonight just about perfect."

They immediately bought tickets for the longest ride, and stood in line. For fifteen minutes they laughed and teased and ate peanuts, and acted like a regular family. Nicki relished every moment, savoring it, and imprinting everything about Jared, about the night, on her memory.

"We can squeeze you into the next cutter, sir, if that's okay," the attendant said when they were at the head of the line, "but I'll have to put your daughter in the front seat, with the two ahead of you."

"Fine." Jared stepped back for his daughter and Nicki to precede him.

A driver, wearing a dark overcoat and a tall stovepipe hat, pulled the red cutter next to the platform where they waited. Two huge Belgian horses stamped impatiently, their rumps quivering. The breath from their nostrils curled in the cold night air.

The attendant seated the two college students ahead of them, then swung Madison up and into the front seat beside them. She was ecstatic and waved over her shoulder at Nicki and her dad.

"The back seat's kind of small," the attendant apologized, offering Nicki his hand.

She stepped down into the floor of the cutter and realized, what with Jared's long length, it was going to be a very tight fit. When he stepped in behind her, his knee bumped her thigh, making her sway.

"Sorry," he said, his hand going to her elbow to steady her.

"I'm fine," she said, trying to repulse the feelings he'd elicited. "Really."

She sat, smoothing her coat, and Jared awkwardly wedged himself in beside her. His wide shoulders seemed to have no place to go. "Um..." He lifted an arm over her head, resting it on the back of the seat. "How's that?"

The space opened up, and their bodies instinctively adjusted, melding together on the tiny button-tufted seat. Thigh against thigh, his chest pinned to her side. The heavy weight of his forearm protectively circled her, and his gloved hand dangled just above her breast. "Fine," she replied, unconsciously using his pat response, and wiggling deeper into the seat. "You sure you have enough room?"

He nodded. She fit beneath his shoulder as though she belonged there, he mused, studying her bent head, the sensuous curve of her mouth.

"A lap robe, sir," the attendant offered, automatically putting it over their laps and tucking it firmly around them.

The sense of intimacy increased. Their combined body heat rose uncomfortably.

In front of them, Madison again turned on the seat. "Oh, Daddy, isn't this fun?"

His face felt tight, his smile freezing in place as he nodded. His body teemed with heat as his desire for Nicki became a driving force that addled his mind and pushed his imagination into overdrive.

His fingertips brushed the red wool coat, dangerously

close to the peak of her breast. Beneath his hand, he felt Nicki stiffen.

"Peanut shells," he explained.

Nicki's shoulders relaxed.

The double-breasted coat offered a mere hint of the curvy front of the woman nestled against him, but Jared's mind's eye envisioned the swing of her breasts and the dark, inviting valley between them. He remembered her warmth, her softness. It was agony to sit this close and to treat her with such casual indifference.

The driver cracked the whip, mostly for show, and yelled, "Hey up, Belle! Clementine!"

The sleigh lurched forward and Nicki's head whiplashed, bouncing off his forearm.

The circle of his arm tightened, and he became vaguely aware of the cold air rushing against his face, the oppressive warmth beneath the lap robe.

"Oh, Jared," Nicki breathed, "look."

He followed the direction of her gloved hand to an elaborately decorated gingerbread house beside the trail. The air became intoxicatingly heavy with the lingering scent of ginger and spices. He leaned closer, to her side, and added a delightful whiff of herbal shampoo to the mix. He didn't notice the exquisite siding of mock gumdrops and lemon drops and peppermint twists, but saw that, up close and under the light, Nicki's hair was a curious color combination of mocha and maple.

She turned to him, and a wispy length of her hair brushed his sleeve. Without thinking, he reached over to smooth it, stroking the fine curls back into place.

Her expression changed. Self-consciously threading her fingers through her hair, she tried to finger comb the curls. "I should have worn a hat," she muttered, her brow puzzled.

He was inordinately glad she hadn't.

The driver urged the horses to the right, onto the established riding trails in the accompanying park. They rode for a quarter of a mile into the heart of the woods. Snow crunched beneath the runners as the noisy activity of the zoo disappeared behind them. They entered a clearing, and the rolling snow resembled a vast white tundra.

"Look up," Jared whispered against Nicki's temple.

Nicki did. Her head dropped back against his arm, and her lips parted, her mouth forming a round, silent "Oh."

A million stars flickered like strobe lights in the blue-black sky. For as far as the eye could see, there was only the incredible magnificence of nature. Trees stood like sentinels to the sky, their dark canopy protecting the endless carpet of pristine-crystal snow.

"I've never seen anything so beautiful," Nicki said, her voice filled with wonder.

Jared scanned her perfect features. "Neither have I," he said truthfully. He wanted to kiss her so badly that he physically ached.

It would be so easy, so painless. To fall off the wagon— or, in this case, a sleigh—for a millisecond in time. He imagined floundering in the powder-soft snow, her body beneath him. Her laughter as they wrestled, teasing each other with handfuls of cold snow and warm, sensuous kisses.

As they left the glade Jared regretted their return to civilization. It was so much better to be set apart, to be isolated and freed from the burdens that gripped him. The two minutes he'd spent in the glade, feeling warm and cold at the same time, were liberating. No onlookers, no memories, no hopes, and no future. Just the incredible sense of the present, and all it offered.

He should have taken advantage of it. He should have kissed her, and touched her, and fate be damned.

They whisked past the toy village, and the pond where skaters made figure eights on the ice.

"I never got to do things like this when I was growing up," Nicki confided, snuggling deeper under the lap robe.

Jared grimaced, and barely heard, convinced she had no idea of the discomfort her stirrings created for him.

"As I mentioned earlier, after my dad left my mom worked as a waitress. We always had a lot of leftovers at our house, but not much else. Certainly not money. We didn't do things like this." He smiled, but only because she'd made light of it. "My mom married again, though, when I was in college. And he was the nicest guy. Good-hearted and generous. He kind of rekindled my faith in the opposite sex."

Jared glanced down at her. "You still keep in touch with him?"

"Well, no...that's the sad part of the story," she said. "He was a trucker, and the first year they were married he was killed when his rig overturned outside of Atlanta. My mom was just devastated. It's what made her move here to Winter Park. To get another job.... To keep busy...you know."

"I'm sorry, Nicki. It surprises me, every time I learn how much has happened to you."

"But that was a wonderful year, and I'll never regret any of it. Joe and my mom would have loved a sleigh ride like this."

Jared briefly let his forehead slip against hers. "Then we'll enjoy it for them," he promised, "and for my parents who couldn't."

"Couldn't? What do you mean?"

He lifted a shoulder. "I was a late-in-life child, and my parents were old school. They had a reputation to protect and an impression to honor. They didn't do much in public; they didn't like to be seen anywhere but at the country club and within their closed circle of friends. My dad used to joke that he employed half of Winter Park, he couldn't afford to know them."

"I see," she teased. "That's where you get your tough-guy attitude."

"Tough guy, hell. That's business acumen." The clip-clop of the Belgians slowed and Jared sensed their ride was about to end. He didn't want that, he wanted to go around forever. "Think we should go around again?"

"No, I might tell you more of my secrets," Nicki said. "I don't know what makes me talk so much around you. I've probably told you far more of my past than you ever wanted to know."

"Actually, I enjoy it. A little insight in what brought you to me, on that street corner, all those weeks ago."

"Foolishness is what brought me there. I shouldn't have been so stubborn to hold out for the bus, I know that now. I should have called a cab, or—"

"No, I'm glad you did. If you hadn't, we wouldn't be sharing this sleigh ride. And, if I remember correctly, you promised me your sleigh was going to come in. Well, St. Nick," he said, looking around, "I guess it did."

Chapter Ten

They wandered into the gift shop, only because they were reluctant to see the evening end.

"Look at this, Madison," Nicki said, "crayons in the shape of all the zoo animals. There's a giraffe, an elephant, a bear. Even a penguin."

Madison gave the crayons a cursory glance, but kept turning the revolving rack of stickers. Nicki guessed that Madison was getting tired, and started to make the move to get her toward the door. Jared had run into an old high school friend and was visiting with him.

"Shall we zip up our coats, Maddy? Call it a day?"

"No. I want to go over there, to see the stuffed animals," she whined.

Nicki shot Jared a glance. He was still visiting, and oblivious to the fact Madison was wearing down. What could it hurt to keep her busy? "Okay. A few minutes then."

They wandered down aisles and aisles of plush pets. Big ones, small ones, everything, in every color.

"Oh, m'gosh!" Madison crooned. "Look at this teddy bear. I love him...oh, Nicki, look." The bear was big enough to sit on, and Madison promptly did so, perching on his leg and cuddling against his plaid vest.

"Maddy," Nicki warned, "you probably shouldn't—"

"I want this teddy bear," Madison said plaintively.

Nicki turned over the tag, wondering if the massive plush toy was even for sale. "Maddy, this is really a lot of money."

"So what? My daddy's rich. He can buy it for me. He can buy me anything I want!" Madison's voice rose, drowning out the other shoppers.

Nicki flushed. "Maddy. You're being loud."

Maddy glared at her.

They were at a standoff and Nicki knew it was up to her to get the child out of the pique. "Come on," she said softly. "Let's go find your daddy."

Madison shook her head and clung to the bear for dear life.

Nicki debated, fully aware that Jaws of Life rescue tools wouldn't be able to pry Maddy loose. "Madison, Christmas is coming and you never know what surprises Santa Claus has for you. Be a good girl now, and—"

"What's up?" Jared said from behind her right shoulder.

"I want this bear!" Madison demanded.

"She seems to have this idea that—"

"I'll play with it, Daddy. Really."

He laughed. "Madison, that bear wouldn't even fit in my car. You'd need a truck to haul it home."

Madison's mouth screwed up into a pout and one tear dribbled from the corner of her eye. "I want it. I never wanted anything so much in my whole life. Daddy...please, I'll be good and I'll never ask for anything again."

"Madison, no. Not tonight."

She kicked her feet, her heels banging against the cement floor. "If you loved me, you'd get it for me!" she hollered.

Nicki's stomach dropped, and she instinctively stepped back and out of the way. Jared's lips went white, his mouth set in a hard line.

Behind them, an older woman sympathized, "Someone's had a little too much fun."

It must have been the combination of statements that made Jared pluck his child off the bear in one fell swoop. She screamed and flailed her arms, twisting and kicking. "Nobody blackmails me, Madison," he said in a flat voice, "not even you. The answer is no. I am not buying you a five-hundred-dollar bear." Madison threw her head back and cried and screamed until she was red in the face. "Come on," Jared said to Nicki, "let's get out of here."

Nicki scrambled to pick up mittens, and hats, and the packages of candles and gingerbread and Christmas ornaments Madison had kicked aside. She hurried to catch up with Jared, but he bypassed the throng of zoo-goers checking out at the cashiers' stations and made a wide loop to the exit. Everyone turned to stare. Madison wailed louder; Jared ducked his head.

Then Madison dealt the final blow. "I want my mommy!" she screamed, still kicking. "If my mommy was here, she'd buy it for me! I hate you, I hate you, I hate you!"

The walk to the car was agonizingly long. Jared opened the back door and deposited his sniffling, sobbing bundle on the back seat as if she were a sack of potatoes. He strapped her in, then shook his finger in her face. "Don't you ever try that again," he warned. "Temper tantrums will get you nothing. Nothing. That was an unreasonable request and it put a bad ending to an otherwise good night. If you ever do something like that again, I'm going to bring you home and sit you down on a time-out chair and you're going to stay there until you know how to behave. Do you understand me?"

For a reply, Madison nodded and hiccuped through her tears.

With dark fury shadowing his brow, Jared slammed the back door. Nicki, standing at the passenger side door, looked over the roof at him. Wondering if she should say something or just keep quiet, she fidgeted.

"Consider this the last family outing for a while," he said coldly.

"I never imagined it would turn out like this," she murmured.

Air whistled through his clenched teeth, and he momentarily looked away before shifting back to face her. "Neither did I," he said finally. "Neither did I."

Thursday was Irene's night off, and Jared had come to expect cold cuts or leftovers. When he'd been married to Sandra, Thursdays were designated as their night out because she didn't cook—and she'd made it perfectly clear that she never intended to try.

So it came as a shock to his system to walk in the back door and have his senses assaulted with the scent of hot food. Christmas carols played in the background like elevator music, and a huge poinsettia graced the kitchen table.

Nicki, looking domestic, wore a bib-front apron and was bending over the open door of the oven, a Rudolph mitt on her hand. "You're early," she said, obviously disappointed. "We're not ready."

"What is all this?" Jared spread his hand, indicating the cake cooling on the rack, the roast chicken she'd just uncovered.

"Dinner."

"And I helped," Madison said proudly.

"You did?" Jared looked down at her and knew, because the fiasco last night at the zoo still stung, he had to try a little harder than usual to drum up his enthusiasm. Although he didn't intend to dismiss her, he knew his responses were cool.

"I made green Jell-O. But Nicki said we had to put pears in it, with red cherries. Kind of ruined it, if you ask me."

Jared put his briefcase down next to the poinsettia. "Mmm. Christmas colors."

"It wasn't that. She says we have to eat fruit. It's good for us."

"Really?" Jared slipped off his coat, and dropped it over a chair back. "I'm glad she's a woman who can think beyond peanut butter and jelly or macaroni and cheese."

"We're having blueberry muffins, too. I stirred, but she got to put in the blueberries. Next time I get to. She said."

Jared paused. "It sounds like you spent all day in the kitchen."

Madison looked puzzled. "No. We was just playin' restaurant."

He watched a smug smile slide onto Nicki's face, but she wouldn't look at him, and concentrated on taking the stuffing out of the oven. "Oh, that's creative. Playing restaurant, huh? I hope Irene doesn't mind."

Setting the stuffing on a hot pad, Nicki shook her head. "We got permission first. You know, when you use someone else's things you have to get permission."

"I'm impressed," he commented. "I see there's little lessons flying all over the place today." Unable to resist, he grabbed a fork out of the drawer to try the stuffing. He popped a small bite in his mouth. "Oh, my. This isn't out of a box, is it?"

Nicki chuckled. "It's that proverbial old family recipe."

"Ah." He loosened his tie, imagining Nicki in his kitchen every night when he came home from work. For the past few years, he and Irene just grunted at each other.

"Daddy?" Madison crawled up onto a bar stool, and solemnly faced him. Wearing a bright red sweater embroidered with toy soldiers, Madison absently picked at the gold braid on her sleeve. "Before we sit down to eat, I gots to 'pologize." A ripple of surprise shimmied up his backbone. "I'm sorry I kicked you last night."

Jared was so shocked, he didn't know what to say.

"I really wanted that bear, but..." Madison twined her ankles around the rungs of the bar stool and squirmed, "I shouldn't of acted that way. I'm sorry."

"Um..." Jared cleared his throat, noisily. "Thank you for the apology, Madison. Since it happened yesterday, I guess we'll just forget it. We'll start over fresh today. No more tantrums, no more being angry."

Madison nodded, her blond curls bouncing on her shoulders. "I love you, Daddy. Really. Even after what I said last night. 'Cause I didn't mean that, you know."

Jared stood stock-still. His daughter's innocent declaration had struck its mark, and a corner of his heart crimped. He should have been able to say it, too, but he couldn't bring himself to do it. Not in front of Nicki.

Maddy looked at him expectantly.

Jared remained silent, painfully aware he couldn't bring himself to utter any tender little mercies, not even to his own child. He'd forgiven her for her outburst, what more did he need to say?

"Madison," Nicki interjected, "how about if you put these napkins on the table for me? We're about ready to eat."

Maddy reluctantly climbed down from the stool, took them, and with one last look at her father, slowly headed into the dining room.

Jared scrutinized Nicki, but her face was a carefully controlled mask. Except for one thing....

He fiddled with his briefcase for a moment. "I swear, St. Nick, this is driving me crazy. For a moment there, your eyes were actually twinkling. You want to tell me how you managed that? And I don't mean the eye thing, I mean the apology."

Nicki's lips twitched, the corners of her mouth finally giving in to a smile. Her dimples popped out, and for one insane moment Jared thought she was the most beautiful woman he'd ever seen.

"Madison doesn't mean to be naughty, Jared. She's just relying on the same old tricks that have worked in the past. Unfortunately for her—" Nicki turned to drop a fork into the sink "—they aren't working at this house. I have to hand it to you. Telling her this is a whole new day is the best thing you could have done, because she's free to start over. No guilt. No excuses.''

"Yeah, well, you know where I heard it."

"Where?"

"From you," he said grudgingly.

Nicki's heart skipped a beat.

"You orchestrated this whole little thing tonight, didn't you?" he accused.

"What little thing?" she innocently asked.

"Christmas carols on the CD player, the house smelling like pine and Christmas dinner. Madison wearing her Christmas best, and you wearing an apron and smiling like Betty Crocker over a trayful of heat-and-serve rolls."

Cocking her head impishly, and tilting the tray, she asked, "Oh. Do you like these, by the way? I didn't know."

"Only with strawberry jam," he mumbled.

Nicki's smile widened. "It's already on the table."

Jared sputtered. Then he turned his head. "Wait a minute. I smell smoke," he said.

"Oh. That. We started a fire in the fireplace. I thought I got the damper up okay."

Both of Jared's eyebrows lifted.

"I hope that's okay. You had all this wood out on the patio."

"I usually don't take time to fool around with stuff like that," he muttered.

"The thing is, Madison and I rented this new Christmas video this afternoon, and we thought it would be kind of cozy for the three of us to have a quiet night, watch a video, watch the fire."

"The three of us?"

"Unless you're busy." Nicki wiped her hands on the tea towel, and waited expectantly for his answer.

Jared impatiently tapped his briefcase. Inside were this week's sales figures. He'd been trying to get to them all day. "Oh, I suppose. Just this once. But—" he lifted a finger in her direction "—you really ought to check with me before you do something like this again."

Nicki appeared properly chastised, but he knew—he absolutely knew—she wasn't.

"Oh, I will," she said earnestly. "I promise."

They'd finished watching the video in the family room, but Jared couldn't resist poking the fire and putting another log on.

"Mmm, that fire's nice, isn't it?" Nicki asked, stretching catlike as she got up from the sofa. She folded the afghan and laid it back over the sofa. "It makes me warm all over."

A shudder went through Jared. He could almost feel her hot, supple flesh pressed against him.

Madison yawned.

"Time for you to be in bed, kiddo," Jared remarked carelessly, laying the poker across the fireplace hearth.

"Do I have to?" she whined.

"Yes."

"Come on, Madison. I'll get you ready for bed. Your daddy probably has work to do. We'll let him have the family room and that raging fire all to himself."

Jared watched Nicki herd Maddy to the door, her arm loosely draped across his daughter's shoulders. "Nicki?" He leaned back to sit on his haunches, one elbow propped over his bent knee.

"Yes?" She half turned. Her hair was invitingly mussed, her clothes rumpled from sitting on the sofa with her legs tucked beneath her.

"You're coming back downstairs, aren't you? I want to talk to you."

He noted that she looked somewhat surprised, even puzzled, when she nodded, as if she'd guessed she'd done something wrong and was expecting to be dressed down for it.

Huh. Dressed down.

He'd like to dress her right down to her silk bikinis and wispy scrap of a bra—and then he'd like to keep right on going.

The woman was driving him crazy. Her face floated above the growing pile of paperwork at his office, and had become nothing but a distraction. He couldn't concentrate and he couldn't get anything done. His mind was always on them, Nicki and Maddy.

No, *Nicki,* he revised. Mostly Nicki.

Even now, he should be going over those reports but he couldn't seem to focus, and he didn't even care. He kept thinking of how she'd looked when she'd bent to put the video in. How she'd looked over her shoulder at him, to make sure the VCR was on the right channel. All vulnerable, and curvy and sweet.

His mind had fast-forwarded into the craziest things, such as running a hand down her thigh or giving her a soft, playful pat on the rump. He wanted to touch her so badly it was torture.

And then Madison had made that silly joke about mistletoe.

Right now, he wanted to hang the damn weed on every doorway in the house and meet Nicki under it. He wanted to kiss her until his lips were swollen; he wanted to hold her and bask in her laughter, languish in her scent. He wanted her softness. He craved her creativity, her down-to-earth values.

It occurred to him they should privately change the words to that old tune. This time around it should be ''I saw Daddy kissing Santa Claus.''

For St. Nick had truly made him a home for Christmas. There was a fire in his hearth, his belly was warm and full, and for the first time in his life he truly felt complete—as if his family was around him. As if he were no longer alone.

He was still on the hearth, the fire an intense heat at his back, when Nicki came back into the room. She tarried uncertainly at the door, as if waiting to be invited in.

He patted the spot beside him on the hearth. "Come sit with me," he said.

Nicki's eyes widened, and she self-consciously smoothed her slacks as she moved across the room. "I never expected that video to take the whole night. It's after ten, and you haven't even opened your briefcase yet. I know you've got a lot of work to do."

She carefully lowered herself to the hearth, putting a respectable foot between them. He smiled to himself. Well, he was the one who laid the ground rules, he thought wryly. "Forget the work."

"Even so, two nights in a row, and you did say last night—"

"Forget what I said."

Confusion rolled behind her clear blue eyes. "Jared—"

"Nicki, listen, I want to be a good father. I want to be a good family man. But I haven't had much experience, and I haven't had many good role models, either. My folks were pretty well set in their ways by the time I came along, and Sandra's only concept of family was a joint checking account." Nicki, listening, her head bent, absently pinch-pleated the creases on her slacks. "I probably overreacted last night about the teddy bear thing. I was angry, upset, embarrassed. The whole shebang. I'm certainly not used to anyone—particularly a five-year-old—talking back to me. And certainly not holding me hostage to her demands."

Nicki chuckled, but she wouldn't look at him. "Kids do that. You'll adjust."

"I'm ready to try again."

"Excuse me?"

"Gillette's employee Christmas party is this Saturday. I want you and Madison to come." He could see the hesitation on her brow and, without giving it a second thought, dragged a thumb across her forehead to remove the deep furrows that were multiplying there.

"I'm not sure that's a good idea," she said slowly as his fingers lightly stroked down over her temple.

"Because of Madison?"

"No. She'll be fine. I mean, I won't guarantee it, but I think she'll manage okay."

"Then?"

"Because of me."

Jared frowned.

"In case you haven't noticed, Jared. We're becoming much too familiar with one another." She stopped short, knowing she had to correct herself. "What I mean is—"

He waggled a hand, expecting her to continue.

"Maybe I'm wrong, but…we just look at each other and know what the other's thinking. I suppose it's having Madison in the middle. I suppose we've been in situations where we have to rely on each other, situations where we've laughed together and relaxed together. But I know your tough guy demeanor at the store, Jared, and I don't want to undermine that image, by revealing a softer, kinder side of you. Not in front of your employees."

"Forget that. It's a family event."

"And just last night you said no more family outings."

He snorted, his head momentarily dropping back. "Okay—and I'm gritting my teeth when I say this—but I was wrong."

He watched the lovely curve of her lower jaw slowly slide off center.

"I'm not wrong very often," he qualified gruffly.

Nicki's lips wiggled, and she pressed them together. "Of course not," she said.

"But, in this instance, I think it would be good for me to have my family represented."

"And what will that do to employer-employee relations? I do work for you," Nicki reminded, "and we do have a very casual relationship, one you may not want to flaunt at Gillette's Christmas party. Sure, I pretended to be your girlfriend at the Christmas gala, but your employees think I'm still the hired help, that I simply moved from one job to the next. Jared, think about it. As you said, we connect on…certain levels. Those might not be levels you want to…well, expose."

Dammit. The woman was besting him with his own hard-line arguments. Old arguments, fall-by-the-wayside arguments. He sighed, and resignation made his shoulders droop. He refused to nitpick every little detail, and he refused to ponder the double life Nikki led: a "girlfriend" to his social circle, a "nanny" to his employees. It wouldn't do any good to dwell on the implications, not the way he was feeling. It would only add more confusion to the mix. "Look," he said finally, "will you just come?"

The loveliest, most fascinating smile eased onto Nicki's face. "I'd love to, yes. Thank you for thinking of me."

He *was* thinking of her, she simply had no idea how much.

Chapter Eleven

Nicki promised Jared they'd be ready by six sharp. Madison, who had been washed and curled, powdered and perfumed, was down in the kitchen, supervising the housekeeper as she made thumb-print cookies. With her white fuzzy sweater, black velvet pants, and patent leather shoes, she looked like the boss's daughter.

Nicki, on the other hand, was five minutes late and frazzled. She was never five minutes late, not for anything.

With one contrary curl falling against her temple, she looked like a tag-along.

Although she'd carefully pressed her best pair of slacks and polished her shoes, when she'd looked in the mirror, she realized a dress would have been more appropriate. It was that five minutes of scrambling in the back of her closet that had doomed her.

Jared would be furious, she just knew it. She poked at the curl again, determined to make it lie flat. It popped out like a corkscrew.

Giving up, Nicki pushed up the sleeves of her cranberry-red dress, and wondered who would be there from the store that she knew. She worried about what they'd think—her working in the "big house" with Jared Gillette himself.

Stepping into her pumps she tried to imagine how Jared would introduce her. He flat-out refused to use the word nanny, baby-sitter, or employee. How in the world was he going to explain her away? Especially with the "girlfriend" thing he'd concocted for his friends and his ex, in hopes of gaining custody.

Friend? Companion?

No, most likely as a playmate. Madison's playmate. His playmate.

Reminders of Jared's last hot kiss, his splayed fingers pressing into her ribs, nudging into the heavy undersides of her breast, tumbled uninvited through her head.

She grabbed her purse and rushed down the hall, fumbling with the clasp on her mother's gold bracelet. She got to the landing and tripped.

"Whoa!" Jared said, looking up. "You aren't going to make that same entrance you did in my office a few weeks ago, are you?"

Nicki colored. She gobbled the bracelet into the palm of her hand, and promised herself she'd deal with it later. Then, she took a deep breath, and assumed a regal air. "No. This staircase is made for a great entrance. I intend to take advantage of it. Just this once. To see what it feels like." Trailing her hand down the banister, she took each step as slowly and gracefully as if she were performing in a beauty pageant. Something perverse surfaced in her, and she intentionally criss-crossed her legs, putting one ankle suggestively over the other, and going for the sexiest hitch in her get-along she could manage.

Jared's smile widened. "Magnificent," he approved, and shook his head. "To think I once suggested you hire on as a bunny. You probably would look good in fur though... and nothing else."

"I can't believe you just said that."

He lifted an unrepentant shoulder.

She grinned and shed the facade. "I'm late."

"I know." He pulled back his cuff, checking his watch. "Six minutes."

She offered him an apologetic glance. "I changed my clothes at the last minute." Shaking the bracelet free, she concentrated on wrapping it around her wrist and fastening it. The clasp slipped again and she grimaced, the corkscrew curl practically poking her in the eye.

Jared tucked the curl back against her temple. "Cute. This hair thing. To do it like that, I mean."

She lifted her eyes. "It was a mistake."

"Ah." He nodded. "Some of the best things in life start out as mistakes."

It vaguely occurred to Nicki that it had probably been a drastic mistake to walk into his office to confront Jared over the Santa Claus issue. Look how things had turned out. She'd wound up attracted to him—physically attracted to him, she qualified—with no hope of a future and no reconciliation of her feelings. She laid the bracelet over her wrist again.

"Here," he intervened. "Let me." He took the bracelet from her, and turned her wrist over, brushing his thumb across the sensitive blue-veined spot where her blood thrummed. Between his large fingers the clasp disappeared. She heard it snap. "Better?"

"Much. Thank you."

But he didn't let go of her wrist. "Let me look at you," he said critically, pulling her slightly away. "I have to make sure this family, including the household staff, portrays the right image." Nicki stiffened, moving back; Jared's mouth twitched.

"Is that how you're going to introduce me, as your household staff?"

"I haven't really thought about it. But I don't think anyone will have the gall to ask. Do you?" He lifted a devilish brow, and let her go. "Introductions aren't my only concern

right now, and being late isn't the only glitch. I just got a
call. Santa called in sick.''

She shot him a questioning look. "What?"

"We always have a Santa for the families and their kids.
I think it's silly, particularly when people only show up for
their Christmas bonuses anyway. That, and the couple of
turkeys we raffle off."

"Now that sounds jaded."

"But it's true, and it's tradition, and you can't fight that.
I tried a temp agency to see if we could get someone on
short notice, but no luck. You and I'll be passing out the
gifts, I'm afraid." He paused. "If you don't mind."

The idea came to Nicki in a flash. "Wait a minute," she
said, "Santa Claus isn't necessarily out of the question. I
personally know someone who has a lot of experience."

Jared's head swiveled.

She offered up a slow, sly smile.

"I thought we got you out of that profession," he rumbled.

"'That profession'?" she repeated. "You make it sound
like something decadent. Spreading a little cheer and bringing a little happiness is nothing to be ashamed of."

"You can't very well enjoy a night out if you're parading
around like…like…"

"St. Nick," she whispered, winking boldly.

He stared at her. "If anyone finds out that I fired you,
then had you fill in at the Christmas party—"

Her hands went to her hips. "Jared Gillette. It's no secret
that you fired me. Oh. I get it. You're letting your pride
stand in the way of letting a few children sit on Santa's
lap."

"Don't be ridiculous. I just can't imagine you getting all
trussed up with a dozen pillows, a moth-eaten costume, and
then hanging some gnarly whiskers on your chin."

"And I," she said softly, "can't imagine anything better
than having one last fling at the job that got me here in the
first place." They stared at each other. Jared debated; Nicki

became more determined. "Hey," she teased, "we'll have some inside information if Madison tells me what she wants."

Jared snorted, but Nicki could see that the humor was wearing him down.

"I'm only trying to do you a favor, because I want the party to be a success. For you. Can't you just accept it?" She laughed. "I can't give you much for Christmas this year, but I can give you that."

"Fine," he muttered, "go ahead. I certainly don't want to deprive anyone the chance of sitting on Santa's lap." He leaned closer to her, his breath tantalizing her cheek. "Maybe this is the year for me to have my photo taken with Santa, too."

"Be careful," she warned, "you'd have to tell me what you want."

His gaze went heavy-lidded, unreadable, and his hand slipped to her waist. "I've always wanted what I can't have," he said thickly.

Jared may have cursed the event as an inconvenience, but the party was nothing less than extravagant. Dinner and dancing, and activities for the employees' children. Santa Claus came in as the grand finale.

While Madison was in the kids' corner with the balloonist, Nicki accepted Jared's invitation to dance, and lost herself to his arms. There were times she could never get close enough to him, to the strength she felt in his arms, or the rounded hams of his shoulders. He swayed to the music and she wanted to melt into him, forging herself with him as one, moving in unison and letting the music forever envelop them. They moved to the back exit, and Nicki reluctantly pulled herself out of the lethargy Jared had created.

"This is the best time for me to exit," she murmured against his shoulder.

"Mmm-hmm. Sure you want to do this?"

"Of course."

He moved to the edge of the dance floor and Nicki reluctantly left his embrace, then slipped out the back door to where her costume waited. Inside the dressing room she meticulously fluffed the pillows that had been laid aside for her, and buttoned herself into the red-velvet garb. Jared may have referred to the costume as flea-bitten, but it was anything but. The boots were too big, and heavily padded with foam. The belt was leather, the faux fur felt real.

Wiping off all traces of makeup, she perched a pair of clear-glass spectacles on the bridge of her nose. With the beard, wig, and adhesive eyebrows she was transformed into a jolly old fat man. She practiced her "voice" while she yanked on her white cotton gloves.

Then she *ho-ho-ho*'d her way into the ballroom.

Children squealed, women smiled, and men indulgently moved aside. A hush fell over the crowd.

Jared immediately came up to greet her, and shake her hand. "Santa! Good to have you," he said.

Only Nicki would be aware that he searched her face for recognizable features. Beneath her beard she smiled.

"Glad to be here, Gillette," she boomed, her voice dropping an octave. "Bit warmer here in Winter Park. Absolutely balmy compared to the North Pole."

"And how are things at the North Pole?" Jared inquired, playing along.

Children had gathered around them, and Madison wriggled through the crowd to grab her father's hand, and peer up at Santa Claus.

"Busy. Toy orders a mile long. I've never seen such good boys and girls," Nicki praised, significantly directing her attention to Madison.

Madison frowned, and shrunk under her father's arm, plastering herself to his leg.

"And Rudolph," Jared asked, "how's he?"

Nicki tsked. "Under the weather, and down with the sniffles. I'm sorry to say he had to stay home. He's resting up for the big night. But he told me to tell everyone to be extra good, Christmas is coming!''

Using that as his cue, Jared directed Nicki to the ornate chair set up for her on a platform. She shook hands along the way, addressing as many employees as she could remember. Some pulled her close and posed for pictures.

The next hour was a blur. While Jared handed out Christmas bonuses and family gifts, she talked to the children. Madison covertly watched from the edge of the platform, and was the last to crawl up onto her lap.

''Here's Madison!'' she announced. ''Look at that camera over there,'' she directed. ''I think your daddy is going to want a picture of this.'' Elves waved, and dutifully snapped the photo. ''And what would you like for Christmas, Madison?'' Nicki asked, bracing herself to hear about a great big stuffed teddy bear at the zoo's souvenir shop.

Maddy didn't answer.

''Have you been a good girl this year?'' Nicki prodded.

Madison tapped her black patent leather shoe against Nicki's shin, then she sagged against her belly. ''I tried my best.''

''Let's see,'' Nicki said thoughtfully, ''I have it on good authority that you helped around the house.''

Instead of agreeing enthusiastically, Maddy only nodded. Her blue eyes were troubled, and she plucked at Nicki's white gloves. ''Santa...I don't want any presents.''

''What? A girl that doesn't want presents?''

''I only want to go home,'' she confided, her lower lip trembling. ''To my mom.''

All the life went out of Nicki. She had no idea. None. Madison had never mentioned her mother, she'd never even said she missed her.

''Presents don't mean anything,'' Madison went on earnestly. ''It would be best if I just went back to my mom for Christmas.''

''I haven't had a request like that before, Madison. It's something I have to think about. I usually deal in dolls, and trains, and video games." She paused. "You really miss your mom, huh?"

The only thing Madison didn't miss was a beat. "Nope."

"Then, why...."

Madison's grasp tightened on her wrist. "Because nobody loves me. Nobody wants me around."

A sick feeling went through Nicki. All of the things Jared had done for this child: the room, the books and toys and clothes. He'd rearranged his life for her. He desperately wanted her back in his life—he even wanted full custody. "I think your daddy loves you very much," she said quietly.

"He says that, but he doesn't mean it. Sometimes he yells at me."

"People who love you sometimes have rules. To make things fair, to make things better for everyone," Nicki explained. "If your dad gets angry, it doesn't mean he doesn't love you." Madison listened, but wouldn't look at Nicki. "Tell me about your mom. If you don't miss her, why do you want to go back?"

"I don't know," Madison said, running her finger along the seam on the back of Nicki's glove. "My mom doesn't want me, either, she wants Howie more. But with her, it doesn't matter so much. She doesn't care what I do, she yells all the time, but it doesn't mean anything."

"So you're used to it," Nicki suggested. "Maybe you just need to get used to your daddy. I know you talked to him on the phone a lot when you lived in California."

Madison's lower lip protruded. "Mommy said if Daddy really wanted me, he'd come and get me. But he just sent presents. My mom said presents didn't mean anything. People give you presents when they can't give you their heart. That's what she said. Before she threw all the presents in the trash."

Nicki winced, from the inside out. "How has your visit with your daddy been so far?"

"Okay, but...when I got here he gave me lots of presents—and then he went back to work. He said it was more important.''

"I see.'' She patted Madison's back. "I think he meant that he's always busy at the store…this time of year.''

Madison shrugged. "It doesn't matter. I can take care of myself.''

Nicki's intuition told her the moment of insight was coming to a close. Madison would only share so much of herself and no more. Part of that was because she was confused about her family and where she fit into it. "Well, Madison, here's the thing. I never forget what anyone asks for. I'll have to see what I can do. But…getting you back to your mom is a big request. And I think there's some kind of law about me transporting kids under the age of eighteen across state lines. I don't have enough seat belts in the sleigh, so I couldn't take you. It's something you'd have to work out between your mom and your dad.''

Madison's face fell. "Could you talk to them for me?''

Nicki took the plunge. "You know what? I'm going to mention it to your dad. But I have to tell you that most kids like to wake up Christmas morning and find presents under the tree. Maybe if you gave your daddy a chance, you could have a wonderful Christmas together.''

Madison's expression was positively forlorn. "It doesn't matter. I just thought you could make things right, Santa.''

"You know,'' Nicki said absently, reaching across Madison and her working fingers, to pull her glove back up and over her bracelet, "I'll see what I can do. Sometimes miracles do happen through the gift of Christmas. The thing about miracles, though, is that they're not always what you expect.''

After Madison was tucked into bed, Nicki and Jared went into the family room, to kick off their shoes and unwind after the party.

With his back to her, Jared knelt on the hearth, and struck a match. He'd taken to starting a fire the last few nights.

"So what did Madison ask Santa for?" Jared inquired, his back still to her.

Nicki hesitated, watching the newspaper he'd jammed under the kindling catch and ignite. He'd be terribly hurt to learn Maddy wanted to go back to her mom. She couldn't tell him, she simply couldn't.

"A miracle," she finally, mysteriously, replied.

"A what?" Jared half laughed, rising from the fireplace to look at her.

"Don't ask. Santa-client information is strictly confidential."

Jared groaned. "I know. The five-hundred-dollar bear, huh?"

"I wish," she muttered under her breath, pulling the afghan over her.

The nights with Jared, especially after Madison was in bed, had become so cozy. Sometimes they watched an old movie, sometimes they just watched the news. He'd started putting his briefcase away when she came downstairs to fill him in on the day, and then he'd started inviting her to stay—to enjoy the fire in the fireplace, or to share a mug of mulled cider.

They'd maintained a polite distance, and they'd only spoken of inconsequential things, but it had become Nicki's favorite part of the day. The time when she had Jared all to herself. When she could imprint his strong lean body on her memory, and taunt herself with the recollections, reminding herself of all the reasons he could never be hers.

She yearned to make every moment with him unforgettable so that, when the time came, she would have something he could never take away from her.

He moved behind her, to the telephone table, and she closed her eyes, imagining what he was doing, how he moved. Jared checked the answering machine; she imagined him listening, the way he cocked his head, the way the light would bounce off of his dark hair.

"Jared," the answering machine cut in, "it's Sandra.

We're having a great time in Vegas. But, listen, I spoke to the lawyer yesterday and I've thought it over. I want the best for Madison, but she's just too much for me. She's such a—I don't know—temperamental child. She's got your stubborn streak. Anyway, I'm going to agree to your terms. You can have full custody. We're thinking about spending some time in Mexico and are just going to let things happen for a while, so who knows how long we'll be there. Who knows, we may stay forever. But I know you, you've got your life organized. You'll find a place for Maddy in it. 'Bye. Wish me well.''

Nicki pulled herself up off the sofa, into a sitting position. Her jaw had gone slack and the afghan puddled around her middle. She stared over the back of the couch at Jared.

There hadn't been as much as an inquiry about Maddy, not even a "Tell Maddy I love her." Only "Wish me well."

Maddy was right: her mother didn't want her.

Jared's head fell back, and an odd mixture of relief and fury shadowed his brow. He scrinched his eyes shut tight and shook his head, as if he didn't know what to say or how to react.

Nicki twisted off the couch, and stood. She should congratulate him, yet Madison's request hung heavily in the back of her mind. *"I just want to go home. To my mom."*

"I got my family back," he said finally, sweeping her with an all-inclusive gaze. "I wanted it—but it's not like I imagined. I never thought Sandra would just wash her hands of Maddy like that. As if the novelty of motherhood's grown stale, like Maddy's a burden. Like she's…disposable.''

Moving around the sofa, Nicki tried to make her tongue cooperate, to say the right things. "It's more than…any of us expected," she said. "So quickly. To have it happen like that.''

He extended his arms. Nicki went into them, this time because she couldn't bear for him to read the concern in her face. "I got my daughter back, and she's staying here," he repeated. "This time for good."

She hugged him, convinced he was a good man with good intentions. She tried to not think of how he made her feel, or the intimate things she knew about his family. The best she could do for him was to help resolve the tension Madison felt. She turned in his arms, her back against the broad expanse of his chest. As she stared at the fireplace, his chin rested on her head. Her imagination kicked into overdrive. It did *feel* as if he was nuzzling her hair.

"I'm going to go break the news to Maddy that she can stay forever, that it's all worked out and—"

"No," Nicki said quickly.

She felt him pull back. "Why not?"

She hesitated. "Jared, I know this is what you wanted." Her fingers went to his arms that looped her middle. "I can feel it," she said earnestly. "And I can practically feel your heart beating right through your shirt, but…don't tell Madison yet. I think it might be more than she's ready for."

His hands slipped to her elbows, and he was silent for a moment, then he said, "I detect something. Something you're not telling me."

"She thinks she's visiting, Jared. She came here thinking she was going back someday."

"She hasn't said one word about Sandra. Sandra was never a mother to her. You've been more of a mother to her than…"

Nicki couldn't bear to hear him say it. Her head dropped and she winched her eyes tightly closed. "Jared, you can't tell her. Not yet," she whispered. "Sandra's message startled me. The bottom line is, I get the impression Madison may never see her mother again. I know how that feels, to lose a parent." She paused. "It touches me that you think I can take her place, and I'm happy to do so, because I've come to care about Maddy. I've come to feel like I'm a

part of this family—even though I know I'm not. But..."
Her sigh became a shudder that rattled through her and
made her want to cling to him. "Leave the door open on
all the relationships, Jared, if only for Madison's sake."

Chapter Twelve

Nicki's pleas deeply disturbed him. Keep the door open on all relationships, she'd reminded, for everyone's best interests.

Well, Jared Gillette was a man who hadn't done that for a long time; he'd simply shut everyone out of his life when Sandra walked out. He'd been bitter, angrily burying himself in work and insulating himself against friends and family.

He'd tried so hard to hang on to his marriage. He'd wanted Madison to grow up in a happy, stable environment. Although he hadn't been happy with Sandra for a long time, he would have sacrificed his happiness for that of his child.

In the end, his bitterness became directed against those who had inflicted no pain upon him. He'd been a tyrant at work, and he'd given the housekeeper nothing but stony silence. He'd lost contact with his friends.

Then St. Nick had arrived, with a ho-ho-ho and the assurance that she could deliver a memorable Christmas.

Not only was it memorable, but it had affected him. In a way he'd never thought possible.

He found himself wanting to open up to her, but he couldn't quite find the ways to do it, or the things to say.

He wanted to say goofy things to her.

Yesterday, looking across the breakfast table, he'd had the urge to tell her how well she fit into his life. Of course he tamped the impulse down, and crammed a dry biscuit in his mouth instead.

He wanted to reach out to her, to touch her, and twine his fingers in her hair.

Last week, in the sleigh, he couldn't resist the one soft curl that had been trapped beneath the collar of her coat— and that one blasted lock of hair had virtually contributed to the total erosion of his male hormone system. He'd wound up thinking about how her hair would look splayed across a pillow. His pillow. On his bed. In his room. He thought about waking up next to her, her eyes all heavy with sleep, her hair tousled.

Dammit, what was happening to him!

He refused to be vulnerable, not to anyone, certainly not to a woman. Especially not to a young, attractive woman who had been hired to work in his home. He refused to acknowledge that his feelings were growing, and he refused to expose the inner core of himself.

Sex was sex.

But not with a woman like Dominque Holliday, his conscience chastised.

This was more than that. A feeling so pervasive it filled his being, his every thought. It made his fingers ache for her, it made the blue-black screen behind his eyelids project her visage uninvited. It transcended every trust issue man had ever invented and thrown up as an objection.

This was intimacy—and it was humbling to recognize that he, Jared Gillette, could be susceptible to it.

He had spent so long protecting himself against others, that he didn't know how to extend the olive branch. He didn't know how to fumble through the niceties and cement a friendship that could be firm and secure—without any greater expectations, without commitment or involvement.

And…yet…Nicki was different. If there was anyone who could accept him, his feelings, and his life, it would be Nicki. The woman was compassionate to a fault.

It wasn't just his life she fit in, he thought miserably. It was his heart.

It was up to Nicki to come up with a miracle. On Santa's behalf, she'd promised, and now she had to deliver. She stared at the motley collection of snapshots she'd collected. Jared had left them lying all over the house, and she'd started picking them up, hoping they'd give her inspiration.

Madison at six months, in a stroller. At eight months, her first tooth. At eleven months, her first steps. Madison in her plastic play pool. Madison gnawing on an apple. In nearly every photo was a strange-looking yellow bunny. She remembered it from when she'd cleaned out the room. It was so tattered and soiled that she'd tossed it in the trash, but Jared had plucked it out, asking where she'd found it. He'd taken it to his room, to put with a few of his treasured mementos of Maddy's babyhood.

She shook her head, wondering. How was she going to convince this child that she was dearly loved and wanted? How was she going to make her want to stay, especially with a father who could be so forbidding, so distant?

Fanning the photos in her hand like a deck of cards, she put them in what she guessed was chronological order. Then it struck her, how her mother had done the same thing, recorded all the milestones, framing them for the world to see. It sometimes had embarrassed Nicki, how her mother would display the photos, explaining that this was Nicki in middle school, in her first pair of heels, at her first job, on her first date—but it had also made her feel loved.

The inspiration she had been looking for struck. She marched to Jared's office, ignoring his request to have an hour alone, and knocked on the door.

"What?" he snapped.

Nicki poked her head around the door. "It's really important. Otherwise I wouldn't have bothered you. I know you're trying to get at that correspondence."

He waited, tapping his fingers across the envelopes.

"Could I take these snapshots and have duplicates made? Or make color copies?"

He frowned at her, incomprehensibly. "And this is a life-or-death matter of importance?"

"Sort of."

He waved her off. "Oh, fine, I don't care. Do whatever you want." He stopped, suddenly, and looked at her. "Wait a minute. You aren't going to cut them up or anything, are you? Not another cut-and-paste project for Madison?"

"Oh, no. Of course not."

Relieved, he waved her out of the room. "Go on. I've got work to do."

"Oh, and one more thing…" she went on. He lifted his head, his eyes narrowing. "You know that funny-looking yellow bunny? The one you pulled out of the trash? Could I have it back?"

Jared gazed at her as if he was convinced she'd lost her mind.

"I was going to do something special with it for Maddy. For Christmas. No scissors, no glue, no damage. You'll get it back."

"In my room. There's a white cardboard banker's box, and Maddy's name is on it. It's in there."

"Thank you." Nicki started to shut the door.

"Oh, and, Nicki…" he said, stopping her this time, "what did you do to your hair?"

He didn't take his eyes off his work, but Nicki's hand self-consciously smoothed the curl behind her ear, surprised he'd even noticed. "Oh, I…highlighted it. A little."

"Nice. Very nice," he said, scanning another letter. "I like it that way. If you'd have asked, I'd have seen to it that you used the salon down at Gillette's. Next time, remind me. We can pamper you, you know. I think you deserve it every once in a while.''

Working nights, long after Jared and Madison had gone to bed, Nicki started putting the memory book together. It had started out as a gift, but it had become a labor of love. There was a noticeable gap in pictures after Maddy had left the house. Jared was in none of them. Only Maddy, in a professional setting, at Christmas, or with the Easter bunny, or at a theme park, where she was pulled up against the knee of some cartoon character. No mom, no friends. Just Maddy. Alone.

Well, she thought soberly, that was what she was trying to fix.

She made intricate illustrations on every page, all the time thinking of Jared and Maddy. Her heart was so full while she worked, that she knew she was falling a little bit in love. She simply wanted to please them. For as long as it lasted, she wanted to savor her time with a guy who was hardworking and good, and a child who merely wanted to be loved.

She got up extra early Christmas Eve morning, with one page left to finish—and she intended to make it spectacular.

Until the shouting at the other end of the house interrupted her.

Tossing down the red gel pen, Nicki pulled on a robe and hurried out into the corridor.

Madison's door was open and Jared, dressed for work, stood on the threshold, his hands, uncharacteristically, on his hips.

"No," she heard him say, "you're not!"

Madison's plaintive wail echoed through the halls. Nicki walked faster.

"What is it?" she intervened, tugging at Jared's elbow.

He whirled. "She thinks she's going home. To Sandra," he exploded. "Tonight!"

Nicki gasped and ducked under his arm, going into the

room. "Madison?" she asked. Strewn across the room were Madison's clothes. An open suitcase lay on the bed, and a pile of books and toys and a few favorite pieces of clothing were smashed inside. "What are you doing, honey?"

"I'm packing to go home," Madison answered, poking a pair of socks in one corner, "so I'll be ready."

"Honey, tonight's Christmas Eve…"

"So?"

"Well, you can't just leave us on Christmas Eve—"

"Why not?"

"For one thing," Jared blustered, following Nicki into the overturned room, "there's no place to go."

"I'm going back to live with Mom."

"Your mom—"

Nicki held up a hand, to silence him. "Maddy, your mom's on her honeymoon. She isn't expecting you, not right now."

Madison turned on her, glaring. "You didn't tell her?" she accused.

"Maddy, we don't even know where she is."

Maddy stamped her foot, and a tear dribbled down her cheek. "You promised I could go home! You promised!"

Realization, and a sick feeling washed over Nicki. Her shoulders slumped and her eyelids drifted closed. It wasn't possible, it just wasn't. She'd done everything right, she'd been so careful to not let anyone guess.

"What is she talking about?" Jared demanded, turning on her.

"Madison—"

Maddy started sobbing. "I know," she hiccuped. "I know Nicki pretended to be Santa Claus at the party!" Sobs racked her tiny frame. "I didn't, not at first, not till after I told her. And then…I saw her bracelet…and I knew… and—"

Nicki dropped to one knee, extending her arms. "Maddy, listen to me.…" She reached out to comfort her, to explain, but Maddy would have none of it, and she swatted at her, backing away. Nicki's arms fell heavily to her sides. "I didn't promise you. Not really. I told you that you might get your wish, but sometimes things aren't always what you wish for. Sometimes they're like a miracle, and then they're even better."

Huge, fat tears wet Maddy's face, and she stood, staring at Nicki as if she'd been deceived. "You lied," she said. "You lied about everything." She hiccuped again, and wiped at her eyes with the back of her arm. "And you weren't even Santa Claus!"

Jared was furious. Nicki had never seen him so angry, and she could only guess at the depth of his wrath. His knuckles were white, and dark clouds gathered on his brow. Against the backdrop of his office, with hundreds of leather-bound books behind him, he was nothing less than formidable. "You want to tell me what the hell you thought you were doing?" His voice was lethal, cutting the silence like a knife.

Nicki's breath rattled behind her breastbone. She hurt all over and the pain radiated outward, making her fingers tingle and her knees shake. She pulled herself to full height, to meet him as an equal. "I didn't do anything. I didn't promise her anything. She told me she wanted to go home, and I tried to explain why that wasn't possible. I couldn't just dismiss her, Jared. What was I supposed to do?"

"Tell her she has a home. With me," he snapped.

"You don't understand!"

"She's my child, I sure as hell do think I understand!" he shouted at her.

Nicki took a quick, calming breath. "I couldn't tell you, not at first. I couldn't bring myself to hurt your feelings. I knew that—"

He uttered another short expletive, and smacked the back of his leather desk chair with the flat of his hand. "I guarantee you no one ever thinks twice about hurting my feelings. Spit it out."

Nicki hesitated. "She felt as if no one wanted her. Her mom had Howie. You had your business."

"What!" He stared at her incredulously.

"She told me the day she came home, you went back to work. It didn't matter that I told her why. She just wanted a daddy, Jared. Someone to love her. Someone to care."

"She knows that if she's here, I want her."

"How? How is she supposed to know that?"

"Look at everything I've done for her. She's got everything any child could want—"

"Well…maybe not that five-hundred-dollar teddy bear," she said wryly, offering him a lopsided grin and intentionally trying to put some levity into the situation.

He started to see the humor, then changed abruptly. "Do you think this is funny? Do you?" he demanded.

Nicki approached the desk, resting both her palms on it. "Not at all. Not from the first. But you didn't sit there and hear the things I heard, Jared," she shot back, her blue eyes going steely. "Madison didn't want presents. She said they didn't matter, because her mother told her you only sent presents because you didn't care. You want to know where they ended up? In the trash. Now. You tell me. How was I supposed to deal with that?"

His lips slightly parted, as if he couldn't comprehend his ex-wife would do something that hurtful.

Nicki tamped down her pride and told him the truth. "I don't know a lot, Jared. But I do know how it feels to want a dad who loves you."

He suddenly looked uncomfortable. "What? I don't say it enough?" he muttered brusquely.

"I don't know. But I know how it feels to lay awake at night and wonder what you did wrong, why your daddy doesn't love you enough to call, to care whether you're alive or well."

"That has nothing to do with this situation," he muttered, avoiding her look.

"Sandra hasn't called once to talk to Madison. You've been busy at work."

"Nicki—" he warned.

"I didn't have any alternative," she said, forging ahead. "I told her that she has a daddy who loves her very, very much, and who wants her with him," she said softly. "I told her that because maybe you can't do it."

His eyes flashed, and she knew she'd struck a nerve.

"You know, though, sometimes when someone has their mind set to believe a certain thing…it just takes a little time, a little convincing. I don't think anything I could have said would have made a difference." Nicki intentionally let a second elapse. "Just like now."

She turned her back on him, and guessed he'd lambaste her for insubordination. When he didn't, she reached for the door.

"Nicki?"

"Yes?" It took all her courage to turn back to face him. When she did, intuition told her something had softened his edges, something had struck its mark.

"It's just that…she said you promised her a miracle."

"I promised her the gift of a Christmas miracle," she qualified. "The love between a father and his daughter. It's something you both deserve, don't you think?" She refused to let him back down from her even look. "Now, if you'll excuse me, I have to go patch up Maddy's belief of Santa Claus, and the ultimate joy and forgiveness of the Christmas season. I promised to give you a Christmas, and I intend to deliver."

Chapter Thirteen

Nicki gently knocked on Maddy's closed door. No answer. For a moment she panicked, then she heard Maddy sniffle. She knocked again, and this time opened the door and stuck her head around the corner. "Can I come in and talk to you?"

Madison, sitting in the great big rocker, stared at the window and vehemently shook her head. With the back of her hand she rubbed at her red, wet eyes.

"I'm sorry, Maddy. I didn't mean to disappoint you."

For an answer, Maddy sniffed.

"I guess you've got a lot to be mad at me for, huh?"

Maddy's blond head bobbed up and down.

"The night of the party, the real Santa Claus helper got sick, so I said I'd fill in. I used to do that at your daddy's store, before I came here. So I thought it would be okay."

Maddy picked at a bit of lace on her nightgown, listening. Her mouth was pursed as tight as a rosebud.

"I intended to talk to your daddy about what you said, but then something happened."

Maddy stopped picking at the lace, cocking her head to hear better.

"Your mom called to ask if you could stay a little longer. She thought maybe you'd be happier here."

It nearly broke Nicki's heart to see Madison's watery blue eyes drift closed, her lower lip wobble.

"Well," Nicki quickly went on, "your daddy was so excited to think you could stay longer, that I couldn't very well hurt his feelings and tell him you wanted to go home. He really loves you a lot, Madison. Underneath, he has a great big heart, and he puts you first in his life. Really."

Madison, unseeing, looked out the window, her visage pitifully sad. "He never says it," she said finally.

"I know." Nicki made the choice to take the blame. "He wanted to tell you how happy he was that you could stay longer, but I was the one who told him not to. I thought maybe, after what you told me, you weren't ready to hear it yet. I guess it's my fault, and I'm sorry. But I wanted you to know your daddy really, really loves you. And he wants you here. With him."

Madison snuffled, her thin shoulders quaking involuntarily. "Where is he?" she asked, hiccuping through the words.

Nicki hesitated, knowing she had to carefully frame the explanation. "He had to go back to work," she said softly, "because he had a meeting. But today is his last long day at the store because it's Christmas Eve. You and I have the whole day to do something special, and plan a great night. Because he'll be home early."

Maddy looked positively desolate. She stuffed her knees up into her nightgown, then wrapped her arms around her shins. "I don't want to do anything," she said finally as she leaned back against the rocker. Her eyes were flat, her voice expressionless. "Could you leave me alone? Please."

Nicki's gaze strayed to the tumble of clothes and the half-packed suitcase on Maddy's bed, and had the overwhelming feeling she'd failed. With Maddy. With Jared. With everything. "Maddy? No matter what happens, I just want you to know that I care about you. I've come to love you, and it hurts me to see you feel so bad."

Maddy didn't answer, and Nicki backed up, intending to close the door quietly behind her.

"Nicki?"

She paused, clinging to the door handle. "Yes?"

"I just want you to know…you're the best friend I ever had. But, right now, I need to feel sad. That's all."

All of Nicki's carefully laid plans dissolved. She'd had every intention to make that particular Christmas Eve so special, so memorable, that they'd reminisce about it for years to come. Yes, well, the day would be unforgettable, all right. It would be remembered as the day their worlds turned upside down, and everyone was mad and angry and hurt with everyone else.

Each of them, separately, were alone as they confronted their own fears and insecurities and regrets. Even five-year-old Madison, an innocent child who had been drawn into the maelstrom of adult emotions, adult needs, was suffering.

Jared loved his child without question, but the tight rein he kept on his feelings, his emotions, kept everyone at arm's length. He thought it was enough to provide for his child. He thought it was enough to provide for his employees, and his charities. He didn't know what people wanted most from him was his heart. It was what Nicki wanted most…and it was something she knew she'd never have, because he couldn't let it go. Jared could never match or return her feelings—and that was an agonizing realization.

Inside, Nicki hurt so much she physically ached. The whole scenario had started out innocently enough. She thought she'd just borrow his family to help get her through one painful Christmas, but somehow along the way, she'd fallen for a love-starved little girl and her irascible father. She hadn't just fallen for them, she thought miserably. She'd fallen in love with them.

Jared Gillette, she seethed, how could you? How could you possibly make me fall in love with you, your stormy temper, and your cold, dark heart?

Jared stomped into his nine o'clock meeting and slammed his briefcase on the table. The two men on either side and closest to him imperceptibly moved away. The eight further down hunkered down in their chairs, bracing their elbows and expecting the worst.

He was fully prepared to lambaste them all—and he didn't even know why.

"Who the hell scheduled this meeting at nine o'clock on Christmas Eve day?" he snarled.

Momentary dead silence greeted his question.

"Um, you did, sir," his vice president of marketing meekly offered.

"I did?"

"Yes, sir."

It happened again. Without warning, Nicki's face floated in front of him. The soft wispy dark curls around her face. The dimpled smile. The compelling impression she made as Gillette's most notorious Santa Claus. In red velvet and white fur, with whiskers, and dainty white gloves.

Jared cleared his throat. "Yes. Well..." A vision of Madison's tear-stained face interrupted his thoughts. "I called this meeting to tell you—" he snagged a deep, calming breath, and stared down at his briefcase. It was filled with hundreds of pages of printouts on sales projections and detailed inventory.

He frowned. Suddenly it all seemed inconsequential.

"To tell you," he repeated, his voice growing with conviction, "that there's only one place you ought to be this Christmas Eve—and that's home with your families. Nobody's working late, nobody's staying late. We're closing up early, and I expect you to be out the door. No excuses. Do I make myself clear?"

Ten jaws sagged, and ten heads wagged up and down.

"That's where I'm going to be," he declared. "Home. With my family. You all have a—" his jaw visibly clenched, and he struggled to get the words out "—merry Christmas."

He snatched his briefcase off the table and strode out the door, leaving a stunned board of executives in his wake.

When Jared returned home that afternoon—early—Madison was sitting on Nicki's lap, with a puzzle spread out on the coffee table in front of them. Irene had gone to her sister's, and the only noise in the kitchen was the sound of oyster stew simmering on the stove. A pan of fudge was on the countertop.

He stood in the doorway, unobserved. Madison's hair was pulled back with a huge red bow. She wore her black velvet pants and red sweater. Nicki looked strained, as if the day had taken a terrible toll on her.

He wanted to take her in his arms and tell her it was okay, that they'd get through it. But he couldn't. He felt like a thief, like someone who had waltzed in and stolen all their dreams, all their hopes.

"Hi," he said tentatively, unbuttoning his overcoat. "I'm home."

They both looked up.

No one made a move; they all gauged each other's reaction. Even Jared. It was Madison who broke the silence.

"Daddy, Nicki told me Mommy asked for me to stay longer."

"Actually, yes. She did. I suppose I should have told you."

Madison stared at him for a moment, then solemnly slipped off Nicki's lap. She walked across the room, to stand in front of him. "I can do that," she said, her stoic face creased with bravery. "I can do that, Daddy. If you want me."

He caught his breath, dropping to one knee, and putting himself at Maddy's eye level. "Of course I want you. I'm glad you're staying, Maddy.'' He couldn't believe the crushing sensation in his chest. How had he gotten here? How had he missed so much? What would it take to repair the damage? He swallowed past the lump in his throat. ''Your being here will make my Christmas special,'' he went on. ''It will be the best present of all.''

Skepticism rolled through Maddy's eyes, and she changed the subject. ''We made fudge. For after dinner.''

''I saw it,'' he said. ''You and St. Nick are always doing something creative. The two of you sure know how to make life interesting.'' He stood, clumsily patting Madison on the shoulder, as his gaze flitted over to Nicki. ''Maybe after dinner we could talk?''

''Of course. If you're hungry, I'll start—''

He waved the suggestion aside. ''Later. Finish your puzzle. In fact—'' he heaved a sigh, and slipped out of his coat, throwing it over the nearest chair ''—I may join you with that puzzle thing. After I change, and start a fire. It'll kind of—'' he shot Nicki a significant glance ''—take the chill off this room, don't you think?''

She offered him an indulgent smile, but her dimples didn't pop out, and he recognized it as a hollow response, one that didn't quite reach her eyes.

They went through the motions. Everyone was pleasant, and too polite. He suggested Nicki put a Christmas CD on the player and she obliged by choosing the most mellow, most comforting holiday songs that had ever been recorded. They ate their traditional oyster stew, and took too much time dabbing at their mouth with their Irish linen napkins, and smiling over the poinsettia centerpiece. They finished the holiday-themed puzzle—of a big yellow Labrador puppy wearing a Christmas stocking—and it was Maddy who put in the last piece, then announced that she was tired and ready to go to bed. Without her fudge.

Jared awkwardly hugged her and said, ''Thanks for spending Christmas Eve with me.'' Then he whispered something in her ear before Nicki took her up to get her ready for bed.

For fifteen minutes he stared at the multitude of presents under the tree, wondering how many Sandra had unceremoniously pitched over the years since they'd separated, and wondering what she'd told Madison. How could she have tormented her own child that way?

When Nicki came back into the room, he was still brooding. She moved around the room, cleaning up.

"Looks like you got it smoothed over with Maddy, huh?" he said finally.

"I tried." Nicki crumpled some paper napkins in her hand and bent to pick up two water glasses.

"Do you know," he said, "that I haven't been home this early on a Christmas Eve in the last decade?" He hesitated. "It was you who brought me back, St. Nick."

She straightened, her look quizzical.

"Don't get hopeful on me," he warned. "I can guarantee you'll never bring me over the edge." He patted the spot next to him on the sofa. "Put those down and come and talk to me. Here. Sit by me when I tell you this. Like we're friends."

Nicki paused, considering both his pose and his invitation. "We are friends, Jared. Whether we want to admit it or not, we put that employer-employee thing behind us a long time ago." His gaze didn't waver from hers, but his eyes were as flat as Maddy's had been that morning. "I care about Madison," she said. "I even care about you."

His teeth clenched, the muscle along his jaw going taut. "We need to talk," was all he said, his voice low, husky. "Honestly."

Putting the snack plates and glasses aside, she came to him voluntarily, self-consciously sliding onto the leather sofa. His arm was across the back of the sofa, and she thought about how intimate it had seemed weeks ago when they'd been in the sleigh, his arm cradling her shoulders. A veil of intimacy had surrounded them then, now it was as if this crazy push-pull sensation forced an uncomfortable distance between them.

He didn't look at her, but fixed his gaze across the room on the dwindling embers of the fire. "Christmases were never easy for me," he began. "Not in this house. My family projected the illusion of mistletoe and holly, but the bottom line was retail sales. My folks worked long hours, and they expected me to do the same. We had all the trappings, the house, the life…but things were never fun. After I got married, I realized Sandra had expected something else entirely, and she had a hard time coping with what we used to call the 'Christmas push.'"

Nicki could only imagine; she knew first-hand what kind of Christmas frenzy Gillette's was capable of promoting. They *made* you want to buy, they *made* you want to celebrate, and indulge. Yet there was a lot of hard, behind-the-scenes work involved. "But it was your family's business," she reasoned. "It's what you do. Sandra had to understand that."

He chuckled mirthlessly. "It's not what Sandra intended to do," he replied bitterly. "She was a user. She wanted, and she took. She saw Christmas as a grand way of capping off a year of free spending, leisurely vacations, and jet-setting." He hesitated, and his forefinger rode the ribbed neck of her sweater before pensively, intimately, stroking the back of her neck. It was such a luxurious feeling, making Nicki want to stretch and purr like a cat. "Our marriage was miserable. It had gotten so we didn't even fight anymore. I couldn't get through to her, to make her understand I had responsibilities, particularly if I was going to support the lifestyle she craved."

His fingers brushed the ends of her hair, sending a fluttery, seductive feeling through Nicki. Her eyelids drooped, and she leaned imperceptibly closer to him. "How did you resolve it?" she asked, her voice barely above a whisper.

"We didn't. She took Maddy and left—two weeks before Christmas. I got a note, saying she was spending Christmas in California with her parents, and then she was filing for divorce.''

Nicki glanced up at him, recognizing the pain.

''I haven't really cared for Christmas too much since,'' he said, his voice void of all emotion. ''It was nothing before she came into my life, and pretty much nothing after she walked out of it. Christmas was hard work and drudgery, my loss and livelihood, all rolled into one. I liked the concept and the idea of what Christmas should be, and the way other people regarded Christmas fascinated me. Yet it was as if I was on the outside looking in.''

Her hand instinctively fluttered to his jaw. ''I understand,'' she said softly, tilting his face down to hers. ''Any one of those reasons could make you become the bah-humbug sort of guy.''

He smiled at her, sadly. ''Maybe. But I wanted the most remarkable Christmas imaginable for Maddy. These past weeks, I've had moments when I just couldn't bring myself to participate. The plum pudding would stick in my throat, and the hot chocolate would gag me.''

''We have one day left,'' she reminded him. ''The most important day of all.'' The silence stretched, and her fingertips, grazing the stubble along his jaw, slipped down to his chest, his heart. ''I promise you, I'm going to make tomorrow your first Christmas—your first family Christmas—for the rest of your life.''

''Nicki—'' his hand slipped over to cover hers ''—you have to understand, I've given up on this family stuff. I can't lead you to believe otherwise. It's just me and my daughter,'' he said firmly. ''Sandra was a user, and it's because of her that I've sworn off all relationships. I mean it.'' He took her hand and firmly put it back in her lap.

Inside, Nicki winced. It was rejection, pure and simple.

''This thing with Maddy,'' he went on, ''sending her out here, wanting her, not wanting her, is just another of Sandra's orchestrations. From this time on, my main concern has to be Maddy and what's best for her.''

Nicki knew what was coming, and had an overwhelming urge to shake him. "Jared, listen to yourself. You're not even giving yourself a chance."

"No." He adamantly shook his head. "It's you I'm not giving the chance."

She stared at him, unable to believe it.

"Especially after all you've done," he said hoarsely. "For me, and for Maddy. For the way you made me feel. Inside. Where I didn't think there was any emotion left."

"Jared—"

"I told you I'd pay you well," he said harshly. "And I meant it. But this family thing is really grating on me. After we're sure Maddy's settled, you need to move on with your life."

Everything inside Nicki went cold, lifeless. "Move on...or move out?"

"I can't give you what you want, Nicki. Or even what you deserve. We're playing this cozy little family thing, but we aren't a family—and we both know it's never going to happen...because I won't let it."

She hesitated. "Because you won't—or you think you can't?"

"I know I can't," he said firmly. "I made up my mind to that a long time ago. Before you ever came on the scene."

"Maybe that's the difference between us then," she said, her voice torn with emotion. "When my dad walked out on us, I swore I was going to put people first, that when I had a family to love they were going to be the most important thing in my life. Families, even the make-believe family you claim this one is, can treat each other well. I believe that with all my heart, Jared. I'm only sorry you don't."

"God knows, I'd love to believe you, Dominique," he said, unwittingly using her given name as he pulled his arm away and rose from the sofa, "but it would take another miracle to convince me—and you may be good for one, but I doubt you're good for two.''

With that, he strode into his office and closed the door, effectively blocking her out of his life.

Chapter Fourteen

Nicki raged, throwing the memory book across the suite as hard as she could. It crashed against the opposite wall, the spine hitting with a thwack. Plastic-covered pages flew, scattering over the Persian carpet, the hardwood floor. The smiling faces in the photos seemed to mock her. It was all a lie. It had been from the beginning.

A dry sob caught in the back of Nicki's throat and she dug the heels of her hands into her eye sockets. Hot, wet tears threatened. Swallowing hard, she fought back the urge to wail and scream and lament her plight.

How could she have been so stupid to think Jared Gillette could possibly care? How could she believe that a few months in his home would offer her the family she longed for?

Jared Gillette get her through Christmas? Preposterous.

Jared had shattered the illusion she'd worked so hard to achieve in one fell swoop. The Christmas she had antici-pated and looked forward to, crumbled under old memories and new complications.

He'd had the gall to suggest they were friends. Physically, he'd touched her in an intimate fashion; emotionally he'd burrowed into her soul as a confidante. He'd shared his innermost secret—and then he'd dismissed her.

One tear dribbled down Nicki's cheek, and she fell to her knees to pick up one page of the book she'd slaved over.

Jared. In a pair of khakis and a dark green sport shirt. Pushing a stroller. He was so handsome, incredibly handsome. If a single picture spoke a thousand words, then she could read volumes on how much he had lost.

She sniffed, and a single teardrop fell on the plastic-covered page. Right where his heart should be.

She wished she could heal him; she felt compelled to try. For, in a way, Jared's wounds were as deep as Maddy's.

Yet her miracle, the one she'd promised Maddy, would heal only a child who felt unloved and unwanted. It would never heal a man with the kind of pride, the kind of misguided determinations Jared made.

He'd made one thing abundantly clear: he'd never have a place for her in his heart. Given the choice, he would not allow it.

The realization made Nicki crumple over the sheet of photos and carefully crafted illustrations. In her mind's eye—or maybe her artist's eye—it was as if someone had drawn spectacular little hearts all over her very best parchment. The initials JG and NH were intertwined. Together they had cultivated a masterpiece, and just as impulsively JG had wadded up every memory and trashed it, claiming it wasn't important.

Nicki had only one option; she knew that. It was time to take care of herself. Maybe Jared, in all his ill-conceived logic, was right. It was time for her to move on and out of their lives. With Maddy in the middle, they were becoming too dependent on one another—and every time he shot Nicki down it was like one more arrow to the heart.

Nicki picked up two more pages, fanning them in her hand. She had done all she could for Jared and Maddy. It would be up to them to resolve the differences the years had imposed upon their relationship. It was time to protect herself; she couldn't stick around and fall in love with Maddy.

Like a litany, it kept thrumming through her head. *She couldn't stick around.*

She couldn't stick around to see Maddy grow and change and become the lovely little girl that kept begging to shine through. She couldn't see her start kindergarten or be in the swim class at the Y.

She couldn't stick around.

A shudder racked her.

She couldn't stick around to see Jared ease up from his schedule at the store, or smile at her over early morning cinnamon rolls and a fresh pot of coffee. She couldn't see him wax his vintage Mustang, or grouse about a few silver hairs at his temple.

She couldn't stick around. Certainly not within shouting distance of Jared Gillette—because she'd already made the horrific mistake of falling in love with him.

At midnight Jared crept out of bed and went to the window. Overhead the sky was dark and the moon full. He felt a bit like the character in some oft-repeated Christmas story, creeping around in a nightcap looking for Santa Claus.

Well, he'd found her…and she was sleeping right down the hall from him.

She wasn't in the kitchen nibbling cookies and washing them down with milk, she wasn't pushing more presents under the tree. Right now, she was probably lying alone in her bed, reviling him.

He deserved it, too. He'd treated her terribly. He couldn't believe he'd walked out on her. But he'd had to, because if he hadn't he'd been afraid he'd say something he would regret.

Something tender, and kind, and loving.

Dominque Noel Holliday had brought so much laughter

and love into his house that sometimes it honestly hurt. He snorted, gazing through the leafless branches on the trees outside his window, and thinking how he'd gone back to his office this morning after the meeting and pulled out her file one last time, looking for more insight to the woman who tormented his sleep and taunted his waking hours.

Dominque Noel Holliday. She'd been born on December 17th, a week before Christmas. Last week had been her birthday...and she had never even said anything. It was a date that had gone unrecognized. No birthday cake, no congratulations, no good wishes. He hadn't known...and still, he felt like a heel.

His fingers curled around the blue velvet box he'd laid on the dresser when he'd come home from work. He must be losing it. He'd gone to the fine jewelry department, and pulled out the thing that most reminded him of Nicki...and he'd just taken it. Just slipped it in his pocket and walked out the door. The crazy thing was, he'd never give it to her. He had no intentions of giving it to her. Especially not after he dismissed her tonight.

His thumb stroked the blue velvet cover.

No, he'd give her the sweater, and the bath salts and the hard-cover book. Nice gifts, solid gifts. Nothing sentimental, nothing suggestive. They were things she could carry away with her.

Maybe he'd just keep the piece from fine jewelry, as a reminder of an exceptional woman who had once touched his heart. He'd put it in a drawer, and take it out occasionally. Maybe when Maddy was misbehaving, and he didn't know what to do. Or when the walls started closing in and he had to remind himself he'd chosen this solitary existence.

Guilt rose and ebbed in him like an endless swell of emotion. Nicki was the lifeline to his child, how could he possibly lose her? The past weeks in her company had made him wonder at her serenity, laugh at her sentimental insights—and doing so had fulfilled him: it had made him whole, it had given him purpose.

With Nicki, he felt like a changed man. He no longer regretted a lost marriage and an absent child. Instead, he saw hope. For what could be, for all that could be. Bitterness drained from his soul and was replaced with the sweetest, most remarkable vintage of forgiveness. Burdens of the past fell from his shoulders, his mind cleared.

Good ol' St. Nick. She was responsible for all of it. With her ho, ho, ho and her penchant for a warm fire and a pan of fudge.

A shadow passed overhead, and he quickly looked up, half expecting to see Santa and a sleigh and reindeer passing in front of the full moon.

Nothing. Only this staggering, elusive sense of a Christmas spirit. It seemed to invade his being, urging him to trust, to extend his arms and let the world be his.

He flipped open the blue velvet jewelry box and tilted it toward the light from the street lamp. Stones glittered, and silver and gold tossed inviting sparks his direction.

His mouth went dry; he calculated the risks.

Knowing the odds were not in his favor, he snapped the lid shut.

It was out of the question. All of it. Years ago, he'd made himself a promise. It was one he intended to keep.

Nicki literally heard the pitter-patter of little feet running down the hall to her room. Her eyes popped open and she reached over to the chair next to her bed for her robe. Too late. Her fingers were on it, when the door to her room was flung open. Nicki slumped back against the headboard.

"It's Christmas," Maddy sang, scampering into her room and jumping onto the foot of her bed. "Daddy said we could open presents first!"

Nicki chuckled, relieved to see Maddy's joy of Christmas intact and thriving. She hooked a long strand of Maddy's hair behind her ear. "He did? Before breakfast?"

"Yup. He said breakfast could wait."

From behind the short corridor, she heard Jared's distinctive rumble of laughter. "Can I come in?" he asked.

Her heart wrenched, thinking of how she must look with her nightgown twisted and the sheets bunched around her waist. What did it matter? Jared had already steeled himself against her.

"Come on in," she invited, forcing a calm into her voice she didn't feel. "I think this is the Christmas morning routine. Only I wasn't prepared for it." She tried to turn, to loosen the sheets, but Madison's weight held them down, and Nicki only succeeded in pulling the neckline of her gown off her shoulder.

Jared walked in, his gaze immediately going heavy-lidded and dark as he paused at the foot of her bed.

She gasped and slapped at her nightgown, pinning it in place before it could fall lower, over the peak of her breast. Then she uttered the first stupid thing that came into her head. "I hear you're not hungry."

He tore his gaze from the rumpled bedcovers, her half-clad form. "I think you know that's not exactly true."

Innuendo hung heavily between them. The man-woman thing. The suggestive dance between people who wanted each other, but were so foolish, so hard-headed and arrogant they thought they could defy the laws of nature.

Nicki flushed. She beat back her wayward thoughts and hauled up the shoulder of her silky nightgown, unaware she was pulling it taut and revealing far more of her curves than she intended.

"C'mon, Nicki. I checked. There's lots more presents under the tree than last night. Santa musta come. I didn't think he was going to, but he did!"

Nicki frowned and tried to focus on something other than Jared's intimate presence in her bedroom. "I thought you didn't care about presents," she pretended to grouse. "Or Santa. I can't believe you're this happy about Christmas. I thought you didn't want to be here."

"Well, I want to see if this year's different," Maddy said. "Maybe this year I'll get what I really want."

In spite of Nicki's discomfort, of being under Jared's watchful eye, she grinned, and chucked Maddy under the chin. "Maybe," she agreed. "Maybe this is the year." She swiped at her hair, knowing she must be a sight. Her eyes were probably puffy from last night's scourge. "Give me a couple of minutes to get dressed—"

"Ohh-hh!" Maddy protested.

Jared came around the side of the bed. "Here," he said, lifting her robe off the chair, "wear this." He didn't offer it to her; he held it away. "Maddy? Go down and plug the coffeemaker in, will you? It's all ready. Then we'll be down."

"Ye-ess!" Maddy slipped off the bed in a heartbeat and hurried out the door.

Once alone, the tension between Jared and Nicki escalated. The room was as charged, as electric, as a string of lights.

"I'm a mess, I—"

"You're beautiful," Jared interrupted.

Nicki hesitated, then pushed back the sheets, conscious that her thin nightgown was up above her knees, and that Jared was privy to just a little too much thigh as she swung her legs over the edge of the bed. Jared's gaze seared her flesh with one scandalous look.

Everything inside Nicki seemed to pulse and throb and beg for fulfillment. She wanted his hands on her, she wanted to lose herself to his touch. She wanted to nurture everything that, in the closet of his past, still needed mending. She was his counterpart. Why couldn't he recognize it?

Jared stood rooted to the spot. He shook out her robe, then held it open for her. Gritting her teeth, and biting back the pain, she put her arms in the sleeves and tied the belt, while he solicitously smoothed the fabric over her shoulders.

It was a deliciously provocative gesture. One he didn't mean, she sternly reminded herself.

"Call it selfish, but I wanted two minutes alone with you."

Nicki's heart turned over. "Why?"

"I wanted to thank you for all you've done for me. For us. I thought about it a lot last night. I didn't mean to walk out on you."

She couldn't bring herself to answer.

"Nicki," he said, leaning against her back, his voice husky as his words brushed over her ear, "I couldn't tell you what I was feeling...I wanted to say I'm going to miss you when you're gone."

Hope withered and died. The room went dark as Nicki imagined a world without Jared in it. "About that..." she said, plunging ahead, "I thought about it a lot last night, too, and I've decided to leave as soon as possible. Maybe within the next few days." She was conscious of the way his hands stilled on her shoulders. "I can have my stuff shipped—there's not much of it—and it would be easier for me to find a car in Florida. It's the logical thing to do, really."

"So soon?"

"It makes sense. Before Maddy's any more attached to me. We want her attached to you," she tried to joke, "not me."

Jared took a ragged breath. "I don't understand this fascination with Florida," he muttered. "I could find you a perfectly good job here."

"It'll be better for both of us. We both know that."

"And what am I going to do about finding someone to replace you?" he growled. "Especially on such short notice?"

Nicki did something she'd yearned to do for as long as she'd known Jared. She turned in his arms and, without any fear of reproach, she wound her arms around the back of his neck, pulling his head down to hers. "Because we're friends I can tell you this," she whispered. "There's a lot of cute, perky little elves in Toyland—and they've all been laid off. You'll find a baby-sitter there. I promise you."

"I don't want some cute, perky little elf. I want someone like—"

Nicki raised her eyes to his, daring him to say it. *Like you,* she prodded silently.

Jared's mouth slid off center, but he said nothing.

Say it. Mean it.

"Hey! Are you guys comin' down or what!" Madison hollered from the first floor.

Determination welled in Nicki. She had to save them both from a disastrous last day. "We're coming, Maddy," she replied, raising her voice. Then, turning back to Jared, she threaded her fingers through the fine hair at the back of his head, stopping at the crown. She pulled his head down for a spine-tingling kiss. For a moment the world, in all its tinseled glory, spun out of control.

"Merry Christmas," she whispered, smiling through the tears that threatened her composure. "Thank you for everything. You'll find someone who's perfect for you. I know you will."

Slipping out of Jared's embrace, she stepped into her slippers and headed for the door.

"Daddy! Nicki! Come on!"

"Your daughter's waiting," she advised softly. "You don't want to disappoint her."

It felt strange to turn her back on Jared Gillette. But he had long ago stopped being her employer and had become just another man—the man she loved. She'd love him for a lifetime, even though they only had one day to share. They needed to make the most of it, to relish it, and savor it. Everything would be as wonderful as she could make it, and then she would bow out as gracefully as she possibly could.

At the bottom of the stairs, Maddy waited. "Nicki, guess

what!'' she whispered. "There's a pink teddy bear under the tree. It's not as big as the one at the zoo, but I love it!''

Nicki squelched back a smile. "Really?" Then she looked over her shoulder, to Jared. "My. I thought there was only one Santa Claus at work last night.''

He lifted a noncommittal shoulder.

They walked into the family room together. Maddy was in between, tugging on both their hands. "You sit on the couch, Daddy, and Nicki can have the chair," she orchestrated.

Both adults took their assigned seats.

The bulk of the presents were Madison's, but she trotted back and forth distributing several wrapped packages and gift bags to both Nicki and Jared. When she was completely surrounded by her gifts, Madison started to dig in, shredding the paper and pulling off bows.

"Wait, wait, wait," Nicki implored, stopping her. "Take some time, and enjoy it."

"I am enjoying it," Madison assured, tossing the craft kit aside, and picking up another gift.

Jared chuckled.

"Madison," Nicki reproved, "Santa Claus, and some other people, have gone to a lot of trouble to pick out something special for you. Take time to appreciate it.''

Madison's fingers literally twitched; it was obvious she so badly wanted to rip the paper from the next gift.

"It's hard to wait, isn't it, Maddycakes?" Jared empathized.

Madison sobered, and her limbs went slack. Sitting on her bottom, she swiveled, to gaze at her dad. "What did you say?" she asked slowly, her eyes narrowing as if she hadn't heard him properly.

"I said, it's hard to wait, Maddycakes, isn't it?"

Madison's fingers plucked at a piece of ribbon, and her mouth wobbled. "I remember that. You used to call me that when I was little."

"Right from the moment you came home from the hospital. You were always my little Maddycakes."

"You haven't called me that for a long time, Daddy."

Jared visibly swallowed. "I…well, I suppose I've thought of you that way. Maybe I haven't said it, not out loud. But I thought—"

"It's okay," Madison said quickly. "I understand." She frowned at the gifts around her, as if trying to decide what to open next.

Sensing a lull in the action, Nicki chose to steer her charge in another, quieter direction. "Madison, open this one next. It's really from your father. But I helped. He hasn't seen it. So, in a way, I suppose it's a gift for the two of you." Nicki reluctantly turned over the gift, fearful the significance would be lost.

Madison accepted the heavy package. "It's a book. I know it's a book."

"Mmm. Maybe…"

True to form, Maddy ripped off the paper. "Oh, wow. It's got my picture on the front."

"It's all about Maddy," Nicki explained, sliding off of the chair to join her on the carpet. Maddy turned the pages, fascinated by the elaborate illustrations, the old family snapshots that started with her babyhood and ended with her last few months. "Your daddy had your pictures all over the house, and he wanted to do something special with them."

Without Nicki realizing it, Jared had slipped to the floor beside them. "Look, there's you in the wading pool," he said. "And you, with me at the zoo, when you were just a baby."

Maddy traced some of the photos, and the memory album did a quiet push-pull between father and daughter. Heads together, they pored over shared memories. The very end of the book was filled with blank pages, and a single note Nicki had fashioned in painstaking calligraphy.

"'Dearest Maddy,'" Jared read out loud. "'This is your

life. We have some empty pages left, but I wanted it that way, because we can look forward to filling them with a lifetime of happy memories and good times. You make me very proud to be your daddy. Thank you for sharing your Christmas with me. Love'—'' Jared choked, and bit his lower lip ''—'Your daddy.'''

The letter was met with dead silence. The clock on the mantel ticked, the furnace kicked in, and a southerly wind gusted against the windows. Maddy finally reached over and pulled the book off his lap and onto hers. Saying nothing, she closed it.

Nicki's heart tripped wildly in her chest. She'd gone too far. She'd put words in Jared's mouth, words he hadn't put there and perhaps he didn't want to put there. She'd put Madison's childhood on the line, she'd brought up the past, and she'd spread it in front of them both. She had intended to heal them, instead she'd gone too far.

Still, there was no going back.

''Madison,'' she said gently, ''there's something else...'' She pushed an identically wrapped gift in her direction. ''It's a little something that I noticed in all the pictures.''

Maddy stared at it. Even Jared eyed the gift suspiciously, his jaw thumping with unspent emotion.

Taking it, Maddy halfheartedly pulled off the tissue. A bedraggled yellow bunny ear popped out. Madison's eyes widened. She yanked the rest of the paper aside. ''Foster,'' she chortled, pulling the faded yellow bunny to her chest. ''It's Foster.'' She pulled him away, to survey his pathetic features. ''Where was he?'' she demanded.

Jared straightened. ''I'd packed him away. I thought maybe someday you'd want him.''

''I've wanted him forever,'' Madison sighed, closing her eyes and pulling him back to her chest.

Nicki smiled, thanking her heavenly stars for doing the right thing where this child was concerned. It was her mother, really, who had unwittingly pointed the right direction all those years ago. Her mother, who had known how to love. "Foster was in most of the photos, and I told your daddy maybe you'd like to have him back. You know, Madison, your daddy has a whole box full of your very special things in his room." Taking a deep, painful breath, Nicki plunged ahead. "Maybe someday next week, when I'm not here or something, you can go through it together. I think it would be good for both of you."

Jared's eyes darted in her direction.

Madison's lovely mouth puckered. "It's my miracle, isn't it?" she sniffled.

"It is if you want it to be."

Maddy buried her face in Foster's nappy fur. "Daddy?" she mumbled.

"Yes?"

"I really want to stay here. Forever, Daddy. And I—I want you to know, I think this is the best Christmas ever." She crawled over wrapping paper, bows, and gifts, to claim his lap and loop her arms around his neck and unwittingly poke him in the eye with one errant bunny ear. "I love you, Daddy."

"I love you, too, Maddycakes."

She turned from his hug, to face Nicki. "You promised me a miracle, and it happened. Just like you said. My daddy really loved me—only I never knew it."

Chapter Fifteen

They spent the rest of the morning leisurely opening presents. Madison, who had grown weary of all the excitement, had hurried upstairs, with her bunny tucked under her arm, to set up her new power print doll.

Jared, thinking they were finished with the gift-giving frenzy, claimed he was going to throw another log on the fire while Nicki checked on dinner.

"Wait a minute," Nicki said, removing a small box from the pocket of her robe. "This one's for you." After everything that had happened, she'd had second thoughts about giving it to him. She extended it, uncomfortably aware the box had absorbed her body heat.

He paused, genuinely surprised. "I didn't expect you to—"

"Open it."

Jared hesitated momentarily, then pulled off the wrapping paper, exposing a small blue velvet jewelry box, similar to the ones they used at Gillette's. He stared at it. "This makes me feel crazy. I haven't had a present in years."

"What? The slippers and gloves from Madison don't

count? The magazine subscription from Irene doesn't count?''

''I meant—'' he broke off. ''Something special. A real present.''

''Then it's about time,'' Nicki said softly. ''Especially after all the good you do for other people.''

He frowned.

''I stumbled onto that sheet outlining all your charities,'' she said. ''It was an accident, and I didn't mean to pry, but I ended up pretty impressed with all your good works.''

He waved off her praise. ''They aren't my charities, they're tax deductions.''

''You don't have to do anything, Jared. But you choose to. That's what makes you special. The respite program, the women's shelter, the foster care program. They are all organizations that make a difference. And what about *me?*'' she emphasized. ''You took me in, and made a difference in my life. I'll never forget you, Jared, or what you've done for me. These past weeks have been…'' She couldn't bring herself to say how much he had affected her. How could you describe exhilaration, wonder, euphoria? ''This isn't much, only a it's-the-thought-that-counts gift. But it's something that reminds me of you, and I hope, down the road, it's a gift that will remind you of me.''

Jared shook his head, considering. ''I got you a sweater, and bath salts, and a book. I'm no match for your imagination, St. Nick. The wonderful album for Maddy….''

She tried to laugh through her emptiness and misery. ''Ah, well, St. Nick has a reputation to live up to. Go on,'' she urged. ''Open it.''

Jared flipped back the lid.

Gold cuff links, inset with mother-of-pearl.

When the seconds slipped away and he said nothing, Nicki shifted. ''I know it seems like a personal gift,'' she said. ''But the first night, when we went to the gala, I kept noticing the way you straightened the cuffs at your wrists. I don't know why, but I've always thought of that. I've never forgotten it. I have this image in my head, of how you looked, the way you smiled. Everything. That night left its mark, Jared. You left your mark. I'll never be the same, not after knowing such a remarkable man like you.''

Head bent, he seemed stunned by her revelation, and stared at the cuff links, his thumb absently flicking the mother-of-pearl.

"I think, after I fell into your office, I fell a little bit in love with you, Jared,'' she admitted quietly. "I didn't mean for it to happen. I only intended to do the job. And the Santa Claus job was easy. It was living under your roof, with all these crazy mixed-up emotions, and seeing you and Madison forge a new life together, that made me realize I have to protect myself. Protect my heart,'' she stressed. "Because I'll never be a part of it. This is your family, your life, I know that.''

His hand closed around her wrist. "Dominique,'' he said hoarsely, "stop. You are a part of it, the biggest part of it. If it wouldn't have been for you, this all would have fallen apart.''

"I don't think so. You're a smart man, you would have found a way to salvage it.''

"I did,'' he said bluntly. "I found you.''

It was the closest to accolades that she was going to get, Nicki was certain of that. "I'm happy for you, Jared,'' she said carefully, "love your daughter for me. Have a good life.''

"Don't patronize me with niceties,'' he said brusquely. "Take some credit. You were the one who gave me my daughter back. You gave Maddy her miracle, and the knowledge that she's loved, and that she's always been wanted, that she was never forgotten. You were the one, St. Nick, who gave me my family back.''

Knowing he was sincere, that he meant all he said, Nicki knew she had to content herself with just that much. She'd take his words away, and nothing more. There was no use tormenting herself on what they could have had between them if things had been different, or had treated them to a different set of circumstances.

"The only thing I regret, really regret," she said finally, sadly, "is that my gift to you is only cuff links. I wish I had a miracle for you. To help you heal. To make you believe that people can love again, that life can go on with second chances and new beginnings."

Jared grimaced, and his fingers slipped from her wrist.

Nicki choked back the swelling lump in her throat, feeling that he was symbolically removing himself from her. He was letting her go. It was a silent admission that he'd never ever be able to return her love, or match her passion. This would, truly, be her last day with Jared Gillette.

"Thank you for the cuff links," he said. "I'll never wear them without thinking of you."

With that, Nicki managed a nod, and silently got up to go to the kitchen and put the final preparations on their Christmas dinner. She'd gotten used to the sounds of the house and knew that Jared was puttering around the family room, cleaning up paper, and boxes, and tossing another log on the fire. He was good at that, always busying himself when he couldn't face the intimacy of a relationship.

For the next hour, Nicki worked in the kitchen, determined to make this dinner—their last dinner together—special. She mashed the potatoes with a vengeance, then she beat every lump out of the gravy. When she went in to the dining room to check on the place settings, she noticed that the bayberry candles they'd purchased at the zoo were on the table, lit.

A blue velvet box was on her plate.

Nicki caught her breath. He didn't want her gift. It was his way of sending her on her way, probably because she had revealed too much. A portion of his last words swirled through her head. *I'll never wear them...*

Behind her, Nicki heard him clear his throat. She turned on her heel.

"You told me you fell a little bit in love with me," he said.

Nicki flinched, fully aware her words had come back to haunt her.

"That's a problem, Nicki," he went on, "because I've fallen totally head over heels in love with you."

She stared at him, unable to comprehend his meaning. Was he making fun of her?

"Don't you get it?" he said. "You gave me my miracle. Why, St. Nick, you're a miracle unto yourself. You were the one who brought love, laughter and hope into our lives. Every day I sat down at this dining room table and I knew it was where I wanted to be. With you, and Madison, and all the wonderful, crazy things you two can dream up. I thought I could never risk loving again. But I was wrong. You proved me wrong. God knows, the only risk I can't take is losing you."

Nicki grabbed the chair back for support.

"You can't go, Nicki," he said softly. "I won't let you. I'll do whatever it takes to keep you here."

She swayed on her feet. "If I was in your arms, I'd be a little more convinced," she said weakly,

He chuckled and crossed the distance between them in record time. "Like this?" he asked, enveloping her in his arms.

"Mmm. Yes." She savored his long, lean length, his scent, the soft kisses that grazed her temple, her forehead. "I can't help it, I love you," she said, making the words sound almost like an apology.

"And I'm so damned glad you do," he growled, his breath wisping across her cheek, her ear.

He kissed her then, moving down to possess her, his hand at her breast, his mouth moving expertly over hers. He pulled her close against his hips, his thighs, rocking slightly into her. "I love you so much," he said, "I never honestly believed a love like this was possible. Not until you came along, standing on that street corner, demanding nothing from me but an opportunity.''

"That, and a little Christmas cheer," she qualified, whispering against his cheek.

"You'll have it, now and forever," he assured. "Because I love you, because you make me whole. Because you're the heart and soul of my family."

He pulled back from her, and reached down to her plate, to offer her the blue velvet box. "I got this for you yesterday...and then I couldn't bring myself to give it to you. After you said you were leaving, I had some second thoughts. My last second thoughts," he confirmed.

Nicki's arms slipped from his shoulders but she couldn't bring herself to reach for the box. What if it was not what she expected?

"Open it," he suggested.

Taking it from him, she knew, intuitively, that she held the rest of her life in the palm of her hand. Whatever happened, whatever compromise came down the road for them, she knew she'd spend her days with Jared. Nothing else mattered.

She gently pushed back the lid. It was nothing as predictable as a ring. A gold heart-shaped pendant, encrusted with diamonds, winked back at her.

"Forget the sweater and the bath salts," he said. "This is my real gift to you. Because you helped me find my heart."

"Oh, Jared," Nicki breathed. "It's beautiful."

"When you wear it you have to think of me," he reminded her.

"How could I ever not think of you, the man I love?"

He chuckled and took the box from her, pulling the chain and pendant free. Working the fine clasp, he lowered it over her head, and fastened it at the back of her neck. "I love you so much I want to marry you, Nicki."

Nicki gasped as fingers moved to capture the pendant. It felt solid, secure, so much like Jared.

"Marry me, Nicki," he urged. "There's nothing for you in Florida, not when your family's here. I was wrong, terribly wrong, to suggest you start a new life. This one's waiting for you. It's right here, and it's waiting to be shared. You, me, and Madison. New Year's Day would be a perfect time to celebrate a new beginning."

"Oh, Jared. That's outrageous. You know everyone is going to say this is too sudden."

He laughed. "And why would I care what they say? Right now, my whole board thinks I'm nuts anyway. I've never given anyone the green light to go home to their families early on Christmas Eve—but I did yesterday. Because I couldn't wait to get home to you. You've done crazy things to me, Dominque. I see you at my dinner table, I see you in my bed."

At the mention of such intimacy, a shudder went through Nicki. It was what she wanted more than anything—to be loved in every emotional, physical way by Jared.

"I want you to be the mother of my child," he said huskily, "and I want to lose myself in you, and I want you to bring another baby—our baby—to the nursery, as the ultimate gift, and confirmation of our love."

The strength of his conviction, the depth of his unbridled emotion, undermined Nicki. All of her arguments were swept away by his earnest persuasion. Jared would give her everything she ever wanted, and he would be faithful and true.

"Just say yes," he urged, "for the life of me, just say yes."

Nicki nodded, her forehead against his chest, tears welling in her eyes. "Yes, yes, yes."

He roared with relief, with laughter; Nicki shuddered, sobbing with emotion.

"Daddy? What's wrong with Nicki?" Maddy asked, hesitating on the threshold of the dining room.

"Nothing."

"But…she's crying."

"I know. I've never seen her cry before. Have you?"
Madison solemnly shook her head.

"I always cry when I'm happy," Nicki spluttered, blotting her eyes with the backs of her hands.

"You must be really happy then," Maddy observed.

Nicki choked, and tried not to laugh.

"It's more than happy, Maddycakes," Jared said, embellishing his voice with a theatrical stage whisper. "She's in love."

"In love! With who?"

"Me," he said triumphantly. "Dominique Noel Holliday is in love with me."

Madison's mouth formed a small round "Oh."

Nicki pulled back slightly and bent at the waist, aching to pull Madison into their embrace. "Maddy, the thing is, I love your daddy almost as much as I love you." He chuckled, his fingers kneading her waist as if they were sharing a private joke. "He's asked me to marry him."

"Oh, wow."

"We'd like to be a family, Maddy," Jared said, "with you right smack-dab in the middle. Our little girl. The little girl who makes us a family. What do you say about that?"

Madison ran into the room, hurling herself at her daddy's knees, and hugging Nicki. "I'd say Christmases around here just keep getting better and better," she exclaimed.

"And the love just keeps growing," Jared agreed. "Because St. Nick stayed, believing in us."

"You know what?" Maddy said. "This sounds just like another miracle to me."

"It is," Nicki said, fiercely hugging her new family. "Love is the most wonderful miracle of all."

* * * * *

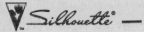

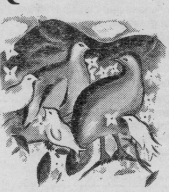

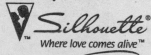

Award-winning author
SHARON DE VITA
brings her special brand of romance to

Silhouette

SPECIAL EDITION™
and

SILHOUETTE *Romance*™

in her new cross-line miniseries

SADDLE FALLS

This small Western town was rocked by scandal when the youngest son of the prominent Ryan family was kidnapped. Watch as clues about the mysterious disappearance are unveiled—and meet the sexy Ryan brothers...along with the women destined to lasso their hearts.

Don't miss:

WITH FAMILY IN MIND
February 2002, Silhouette Special Edition #1450

ANYTHING FOR HER FAMILY
March 2002, Silhouette Romance #1580

A FAMILY TO BE
April 2002, Silhouette Romance #1586

A FAMILY TO COME HOME TO
May 2002, Silhouette Special Edition #1468

Available at your favorite retail outlet.

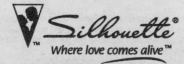

Silhouette®
Where love comes alive™

SSERSFR